W9-CPF-539

The Price of Loving a Hustla:

Maliah & Case

By: Candace Lashell

DOUGLASS BRANCH LIBRARY
Champaign Public Library
504 East Grove Street
Champaign, Illinois 61820-3239

Copyright © 2016 by Candace Lashell

Published by Silver Dynasty Publications

All rights reserved

This book is a work of fiction. Names, characters, places, and incidents either are the product of the author's imagination or are used fictitiously and are not to be construed as real. Any resemblance to actual persons, living or dead, business establishments, events, or locales or, is entirely coincidental.

No portion of this book may be used or reproduced in any manner whatsoever without writer permission except in the case of brief quotations embodied in critical articles and reviews.

For information contact; silverdynastypublications@yahoo.com

ISBN-13: 978-1536936384

ISBN-10: 1536936383

ACKNOWLEDGEMENTS

First and foremost, I want to thank God for blessing me with the talent to write and the courage to share it with others. His grace never fails me. I am thankful for the opportunity to pursue my dreams. To my family, friends, and supporters, thank you for every word of encouragement, every share, every like and every listening ear. I appreciate you for believing in me. To Mercedes, I can't thank you enough for seeing the talent within me and giving me the opportunity to work under your wing. You have introduced me to the wonderful ladies of SDP: You are all the most genuine group of women that have embraced, and motivated me with open arms. I'm so appreciative of each of you!

Dedication

This book is dedicated to every single person who has loved, supported, motivated, and captivated me in any way. I'm the furthest thing from perfect but to still have people who want nothing but the best for me is a blessing within itself! Charles thank you for the ultimate sacrifices for our family. They are greatly appreciated.

My beautiful babies Christian and Carter this is for you! Follow your dreams and always believe in yourselves!

We are brave and wiser because they existed, those strong women and men....We are who we are because they were who they were. It's wise to know where you come from, who called your name
-Maya Angelou

Follow me:
Facebook: Candace Lashell Williams
Instagram: Candacelashell
Twitter: Candacelashell

Chapter 1: Maliah

I had to take a deep breath as I struggled to climb the stairs of a two-bedroom townhouse that I shared with my sisters Kayla, Marquita, my brother, Jaylen, and my mama, Rosie.

Going up and down the stairs had become a chore for me at seven months pregnant, and if someone would have told me five years ago that I would be pregnant not even a year after high school, I would have told them to go to hell, but there I was, waddling and bumping, belly first, into everything. I had just gotten home from my doctor's appointment, and I wanted nothing more than to kick my feet up and relax. I knew that was wishful thinking, because it was always something around the house that I had to do or take care of.

"Maliah, can I do your hair pleaseee?" I looked up and saw my six-year-old sister Kayla standing at the top of the stairs eagerly waiting for my answer with her paddle brush and comb in hand.

"No, but I can do yours." I smiled.
Finally reaching the top of the stairs, I stroked my hand across her bushy ponytail that was bigger than her head. Kayla hated when I combed her hair, and I was not a fan of combing it, but my mama was out somewhere getting high or panhandling, leaving me with no choice but to do it. I was

so thankful that I was pregnant with a boy, because girls required a ton of maintenance.

"Come on, Kay Kay." I said to her, as she whined and stomped her feet. We walked down the hall that lead to our room that the four of us shared, including my brother Jaylen. I had a padlock installed on our bedroom door to keep my mama from stealing our things. I didn't make much at Chicken Shack, so the things I bought, I didn't need to be stolen. She used her entire SSI check on drugs and alcohol and would often sell our government food card until I took control of it. We lived in low-income housing, so our rent was only $76.00 a month, and I was left to pay it along with our light bill.

"Ouch!" Kayla yelled, as I barely touched her head. I felt my son doing flips as I struggled to detangle her hair. Just as I was finishing her last ponytail, a bang on the front door interrupted my thoughts of how my future would play out. I paced slowly down the stairs to the front door. I stood on my tippy toes to see Eriq standing impatiently on my doorstep. I unlocked the door, and he barged in past me.

"Damn, it took you forever to open the door." he said, seemingly annoyed.

"Well, shit, you know I move slowly these days." I said, rubbing my overgrown belly and eyeing the KFC bag in his hand, which caused a smile to creep up on my face. My cravings throughout my pregnancy had been KFC chicken.

"I knew yo ass was over here hungry." he laughed, noticing how I was excited about food. Eriq was my child's father. We had been together the last two years off and on. He was twenty years old, making him two years older than I was. Lately, we had both been stressed because we had exactly two months to figure out what we were going to do with our lives before our baby was born. I couldn't have a newborn sleeping in a bedroom with four other bodies.

I raised my sisters and brother by myself. It was me that bathed them, helped with homework, combed hair, cooked dinner, and did the disciplining. My dad died when I was seven years old of lung cancer. As a beneficiary on his life insurance policy, I was awarded $6000 when I turned eighteen. The money was a lot under the circumstances I was under, and the policy was split between his six other children and ex-wife.

My mama was my Dad's sidepiece. After slipping up and getting her pregnant, he chose his wife and other six kids over my mama and me. My mama was considered weak to me, because after my father's decision, she began to indulge in using drugs and sleeping with countless men. Hell, she had no clue who fathered my siblings. We looked like Dashiki's kids from the movie Don't be a Menace.

I was Cocoa Brown with dark eyes, high cheekbones, and full lips. Marquita had a caramel complexion with long, curly, sandy brown hair and hazel eyes. She looked a lot like our mother. Jaylen was a darker tone, with chinky, reddish-brown eyes, and then there was Kayla. Without a doubt, she was biracial. Her skin was pale, her eyes were a clear green, and her hair was jet black with loose curls. Without knowing us, someone would never guess that we were related.

"How are you feeling today?" Eriq asked, taking a seat on our small love seat.

"I feel okay. Just a lil' tired from studying all night and picking up extra hours at work." I responded, working on my second piece of chicken.

"Well, that's cool that you are able to still maintain school." he said, looking at his vibrating phone. Eriq was extremely handsome, and he towered over me with his 6'2, slender build. He kept his hair cut low, and he had thick waves that he brushed every chance he got. His smooth, golden brown complexion was flawless. His eyes were always low like he had just smoked the best weed anyone had to offer, even though he wasn't a smoker. Needless to say, he looked like someone God himself had sent down to me specifically.

Our two-year duration definitely had its ups and downs. Mostly with me being on the shorter end of the stick. Although, he looked perfect, he was far from it. In fact, his looks was what kept him in trouble. Females stayed thirsty and was willing to go through drastic measures to sleep with him, and a few of them in the past, he has taken up their offering. I always thought that, because I was quiet and spent most of my time preoccupied taking care of my siblings, he used it to his own selfish advantage.

I had broken up with him before I had gotten pregnant because of his cheating. I had sex with him during the break up, and it resulted in pregnancy. I wanted him to get a job before the baby was born, but I knew that was one request that would go unmet. He made a living out of selling nickel and dime bags of weed, and doing auto repairs for people around the hood. He lived with his brother, his brother's girlfriend, and their three kids. His mama put him out when she found out he was dealing drugs. She did not want any parts of it in her house.

Eriq had been insisting lately that I give him $3000.00 to flip. He would always say that, if I fronted him the money, it would change our lives forever. I had made the mistake before of giving him my college refund check to invest, and all he brought home with him was a new wardrobe for himself and me $300.00. This was all the money that I had to try to do the best I could to take care of four kids and myself. I had to really think of a plan to get my own place. I knew I had no business having a baby, but what was done was done. We could only have sex when the kids were at school. If they were home, then we were shit out of luck.

"Baby, I want to talk to you." Eriq said, nervously.

"What's up?" I asked, giving him my undivided attention. He gave me a crooked grin and looked down at his phone.

"What?! Why in the hell are you being so weird?" I asked him.

"I wanted to see what's up with you handing over the three racks, so I can make something happen for us." he said, still not looking at me.

As bad as I wanted to give him the money with hopes that he would turn it into riches, I knew that I didn't trust him enough to give him half of my inheritance. I let out a long, exaggerated sigh.

"I don't know-" I was cut off by a loud banging on the door. Whoever it was at my door was banging like they were being chased by pit bulls. Eriq walked over to the door and looked out the peephole. Without consulting with me, he opened the door. Some cracked out man was carrying my mama's drunk ass in his arms. Both of them reeked of cheap alcohol, stale cigarettes, and ass.

"What the hell!" I shouted out. The stranger walked my mama over to the couch and dumped her on her back.

"Niggaa, youu better have my shiiit when youu get back." my mama slurred to the man. He smiled wide showing off his decayed teeth. Eriq quickly escorted the man toward the front door and slammed it in his face without saying a word to him.

"Heyy y'alll," my mama said to Eriq and me, waving her hand back and forth. I held my head down. This shit was embarrassing as fuck. I hated to see my own mother coming. She was no good to us or herself.

"We will talk later." I said to Eriq with tears welled up in my eyes. He walked over to me and pulled me by my hand into the kitchen.

"Listen Maliah, we can't keep doing this shit." I can't have you and my baby living like this. If you front me this money, baby, I'll make it happen. I won't disappoint you." he said, looking me dead in my eyes. I felt my heart beating faster and my baby kicking harder.

"Yesssssss!!" my mama yelled out. I looked around Eriq and spotted her drunk ass laying on the couch pissing on herself.

He was right; I couldn't live like this. I couldn't let my sisters and brother live like this. I had to put some trust into my man and myself, because we both had to make some shit happen. He was right; I had so much on my plate that I couldn't think straight half of the time.

"Okay, meet me at the bank tomorrow after I get off work, and I'll give you the money." I said. Eriq smiled widely which resulted in his eyes dropping lower than what they already did. My heart melted down into a puddle, then he kissed me deeply.

"Baby, you will have the world at your feet when I'm done. I promise." I wasn't familiar with the emotion I was feeling, but it felt right.

"Let me clean her up before the kids see her like this. Thank you for lunch; I will call you later." I said, wanting him to leave, because no matter how many times he saw my mama in this state, it was still humiliating to me.

He kissed my forehead, and I walked him to the door. I watched him walk to his Monte Carlo and peel off.

"Come on!" I yelled at my mama. She staggered toward me pissy drunk. Don't touch me or anything in this house. Go straight to the bathroom."

She annoyed me so badly that it made my blood boil over. I walked in front of her leading her to the bathroom. I helped her to take the clothes off that she had on and sat her in the bathtub. I let the shower water run on her body. She was so drunk that she laid in the tub like she was in a bed, while I made sure her face was clear of water. I gathered her soiled clothes and placed them in a small trash bag that I got from underneath the bathroom sink. I went into our room where Kayla was sleeping on the bottom bunk she shared with Jaylen. It was so tight in the room with the full-size bed I shared with Marquita. I grabbed my Bath and Body Works body wash. I poured the gel over her body and proceeded to clean her off.

My mom hadn't been home in days, so I knew that a drop of water hadn't hit her anywhere. She was sleeping like a baby while I washed her ass like she was baby. I turned the hot water off and let the cold water hit her, but she was so fucked up that it didn't faze her that the water was ice cold. I cut off the water and grabbed a towel to dry her off.

"Mama, wake up." I said nudging her. I violently shook her, then she opened her eyes and struggled to sit up.

"Come on get out the tub." She held onto my shoulders as she stepped out the tub. I towel-dried her used up body. As I rumbled through the bathroom closet, I found a can of oil sheen to spray her down with. By this time, I was fed up and not about to give her a massaged lotion down. Shit, I needed one, not her. I sprayed the hair spray on her ass and threw her on an oversized, clean, white t-shirt. Then, she slowly followed me to her room and gently sat on the bed. She looked at me and smiled a wide, creepy smile, displaying her yellow teeth.

"Youu are so good to us Lady Bugg; youu are special." she slurred. Even though she was drunk, and I still had to go clean piss off the couch, I smiled back at her. Under the circumstances, I was glad that she acknowledged my efforts.

"Lay down, Mama, get some rest." I said, putting the blanket over her. I stared at her for a brief moment. I remember her being so beautiful and full of life. She wasn't always this way, but now, I watched as life slowly ate away at her. All she ever wanted was to be loved, but sought it in all the wrong places. She needed love from men in her mind . Men that only used, abused, and manipulated her weak mind. A tear slid down my face. She didn't understand how much we loved her… how much we needed her. I kissed her cheek before I left the room to walk down the stairs for the 100th time that day and began to clean up the house and prepare dinner. Shit was hard, and in two months, it was about to get harder.

Chapter 2: Maliah

I had dropped the last basket of wings for my shift, and I was headed to the break room to throw in my apron. I had to meet Eriq at my bank, so that I could make the withdrawal and give him the money. On my way out the door, I ran into April, who went to high school with me.

"Hey, Maliah!" she said overly excited. I never rocked with her like that, so I was confused as to why she was so thrilled to see me.

"Hey April." I waved and kept walking toward the door.

"How have you been?" she asked, chewing her gum and playing with her hooped earring.

"I've been good; it was nice seeing you." I said flat. I had to get to the bank and back home in time to meet Kayla and Jaylen at the bus stop. I didn't have time to converse with this bitch. She was always messy, and I wasn't in the mood for it.

"You getting big; yo baby gon' be so cute girl. Eriq is fine." she giggled.

"Yea, he will be fine just like My Man." I huffed and stormed out the door not giving her the chance to take me there.

I made it to my Ford Focus and sped to the bank. I pulled up next to Eriq in my bank's parking lot and watched him step out his car and over to mine to open my door. My stomach knotted, because I couldn't believe I had agreed to give him my money. He had his snapback pulled down so low, I could barely see his sexy eyes, but the knots went away at the sight of him. The hold he had over me was tight.

"Hey Bae, how was work?" He asked.

"It was okay." I snapped at him.

I was still pissed off at April's appearance at my job. Eriq learned a long time ago that, when I was pissed off, to stay out of dodge. He helped me out of the car and followed me into the bank. He took a seat in the lobby while I handled my business. I was happy he did, because I didn't want him to hear me conduct my business. I was sitting on a little over $7000.00 dollars, and I didn't need him overhearing any more than I wanted him to know. I finished off the transaction and walked over to Eriq handing him the envelope full of money. He smiled and tucked the money in his pocket. After we left the bank, he followed me to my house.

I had exactly an hour and a half to get some before the bus dropped the kids off, so I rushed in the house with Eriq hot on my ass. With me pulling overtime and drowning in classes, I hadn't had sex in two weeks, and I was ready to explode. I laid a blanket down on the couch, and Eriq wasted no time tugging at my pants.

"Wait baby, I got to pee." I whined.

"Damn, you gotta pee right now?" he asked, hanging his head while looking at me.

"Yes I have to now." I had to pee every six seconds, because the baby was sitting on my bladder. He helped me off the couch, and I wobbled my ass to the bathroom.

"Hurry up!" Eriq yelled. I wasted no time peeing and giving myself a quick wash up. When I made it to the couch, he had his pants and boxer briefs off, and his thick, long dick was standing up waiting for me to get back. I laid back down on the couch, and he tugged my pants down again. He was successful at getting them off, and I was ready, as he began to kiss on my thighs.

"Baby no, the doctor said you can't go down on me any more during the pregnancy." I announced hot and bothered.

"What?" he asked with his face all screwed up. I was his favorite meal, and I was now telling him he had to starve until after the baby.

"You just can't." I said, not wanting to elaborate and only wanting the dick. I must have pissed him off with that announcement, because he didn't kiss me anywhere else. He positioned himself on top of me with no further foreplay, which was actually fine with me, because I was horny and leaking already. He pushed his way inside, and it drove me crazy how he struggled a little to get in every time we had sex. My baby was well-endowed.

"Unhhh," I moaned loudly. I was so wet you could hear him dipping in and out of me. I wish I could see my juices coat him, but my huge belly stood in the way. Instead, I got off seeing him look down, him entering in and out of me, and just watching him throw his head back in ecstasy.

"My pussy so good," he groaned. He lightly pinched my nipple, causing me howl in pleasure. He picked up his pace, and all you heard was me screaming and him slamming into my kitty.

I knew I was going to be sore when he was done. I felt all the tension that had built up in me rise, as I rode him from underneath. He gripped my hips to catch my rhythm, because I was laying it good on him. He locked eyes with me, and I could feel the passion and love radiating off of him. He leaned in to kiss me, then we tongued each other down not missing a beat of our lovemaking. Eriq's sex was fire. He was the only dude who had had any of this, but I was almost sure that this was the best it could get.

"Don't you ever let a soul feel this shit." he grunted. I looked him in the eyes and nodded my head in agreement with him. I was paralyzed and scared to say anything to throw off the focus I had gained that lead me to almost being in euphoria.

"Unhhhh yessss, Daddyyy." my toes curled. My nails clawed at his back, as my pussy creamed, and he kept hitting it. It wasn't long before he let loose inside of me and sat in between my legs struggling to regain his composure. I looked at the time on my phone, and I had twenty minutes to get myself together before the kids would be home. I took a quick ten minute shower and began to prepare them an after school snack. Eriq stood in the doorway smiling at me.

"My son is so blessed to have yo fine ass as his mama." he said smiling. I hated when he gave me compliments. I would turn bright red and have this stupid smile on my face that I couldn't wipe off no matter how hard I tried.

"Don't start." I said smiling. He knew how bad I hated him to put me on the spot.

"Naw forreal." He said, walking closer to me. "You do so much for everyone, I can't wait to take care of you and our baby." All I could do was smile and hang onto his words. I couldn't remember ever being taken care of.

Since I was a little girl, I would wipe tears from my mom's eyes and console her when she was sad that my dad didn't want us in his life. From her having more babies and me having to step up to play mama, no one had ever gave me this type of attention. So for him to tell me this, made me want to hang onto his word.

"I want you to know, Maliah, that I love you more than anything in life, and everything that I put you through was a part of me growing up to be the man you and my son need me to be. I'm going to help you raise your sisters and brother. I'm going to be all y'all need to be straight."

I began to shed tears. I was pregnant and already emotional, but to hear the man I love want better for my family touched me with promises that, at this point, I could only dream of experiencing.

Eriq didn't leave my house until late that night. We played Twister with the kids, he played video games with Jaylen, and then we chilled eating pizza. These were the types of nights that made me forget the situation we were in. It warmed my heart to see the kids and Eriq smiling, and it made me feel that everything would be alright. In this moment we shared together, we were good.

The next morning, I had to be at school at 8:00 am. My morning routine consisted of laying out Kayla and Jaylen's clothes for school, making lunches, and making sure Marquita was up to send them off to school before she went to school. We all had to help make life a little easier for one another.

My mama hadn't been home in a week, and I was always afraid that someone was going to show up here and tell me she was dead. I brushed my teeth in the shower while rubbing my belly. I was in a great mood, and I wasn't letting thoughts of her ruin my day.

School went by slow, and I had a hard time focusing on anything my professor was saying. I kept checking my phone looking forward to Eriq texting me back Good Morning like he did every morning. It was now noon, and I was done with my classes and still no text from Eriq. *This is weird.* I thought. He always texted me.

I treated myself to lunch to take my mind off of him for the moment. As I sat down in the diner studying my notes from class, I felt someone walking toward me. I looked up to see Case headed my way. I knew Case from around the way. He was a prodigy in my hood and big in helping a lot of the elderly and single women in our area. Although I never talked to him, I would see him, speak, and always keep it moving.

He was older than me. I knew not by too much, but everything about him screamed mature and experienced. I could smell his expensive cologne pouring off his skin. He was black as night, with a neatly trimmed goatee. He had shiny, black hair with a lineup that looked like Jesus edged him up himself. His pretty white smile with one deep dimple on his right side was enough to have you in the daze. He wore all black shorts, with a black t-shirt and black Valentino sneakers. His diamond earring danced on his earlobe, and his Jesus pieces around his neck looked like the Heavenly gates were opening, because they shined so brightly.

"Yo, what's going on Lady?" He asked, pulling up a chair without asking me if I wanted company.

"Hey." I spoke nonchalantly.

"Why is your pretty self-sitting alone?" He questioned.

"I'm studying, and I need to be alone." As fine as he was, I needed to study, and I needed him out my face before word got back to Eriq that I was entertaining him. Just then, the waiter walked up with my glass of water and grilled chicken breast.

"What the hell? Who goes out to eat and just orders a breast? No bread, or nothing?" Case questioned studying my plate. I couldn't contain myself from laughing uncontrollably.

"I don't want anything else; I'm picky these days." I rubbed my belly.

"I'm saying, how do you order that? Aye' lemme get a grilled chicken sandwich minus everything but the breast?" He asked me with a confused face. I was now laughing so hard, I couldn't breathe.

"Get yo crazy ass away from my table." I said, dabbing my eyes with the napkins.

"But for real, you need to feed the baby a little better than that." He said still eyeing my plate.

"He is good; we are good." I said to him.

I had heard from my neighbor Ayesha that Case told all of the local drug dealers in our hood not to serve my mama. He was heavy in the streets, and his money was longer than a 50 ft. pole. I'm sure that when a feign came his way, he didn't turn down money, but to hear he had my mama turned down numerous times made me appreciative of what he'd done.

"I heard my mama was trying to cop on your territory; I appreciate you declining." I changed the subject to a more serious matter. I was thankful he didn't feed her habit. I could tell it threw him off guard, and that he didn't know that I knew about what he'd done.

"Naw, no need to thank me for that. Yo mama is cool people. I want to see her get clean and get that monkey off her back, so if I can help her, that's what I'm going to do." He said with sincerity.

"Thank you." I managed to say. He was tugging at all of my sensitive emotions.

"I want the best for you, too." He said throwing me off guard. I had been seeing Case most of my life, but he was the guy you would lust over but never pursue. His name was always in some shit, and I was always opposed to drama. I began to cut my chicken breast into small dices.

"I told you I am good, but I appreciate your concern." I said, before taking a bite of my food.

"Yea, so yo baby daddy treating you right? Taking care of home?" He questioned.

I nodded my head yes without opening my mouth. Talking about Eriq wasn't up for conversation, and mentioning him only shifted my thoughts back to the fact I hadn't heard from him all day.

"I have a strong feeling I can treat you better. I hope he is a smart man, because if he ever drops the ball, I'll be there to play all positions." He said, staring into my eyes. I don't know why, but his words sent chills up my body. I had never held a conversation with him before, and he was now in my face talking like this while I stuffed my face with food at seven months pregnant.

"Case, I have to get back to studying." I said, blowing off his comment.

"Okay, I'll let you get back to your studies; I'll see you around, Maliah." He stood up and pushed his chair in not taking his eyes off of me, causing me to be uncomfortable.

He finally walked away. *Damn, that was weird.* I thought.

Chapter 3: Case

After I left the diner choppin it up with Maliah's fine ass, I came to chill in the hood. I had been seeing her since we were young as hell, but it wasn't until recently that she had my full attention. She was like that good girl that a nigga would stay overlooking, because it was too many hoes throwing it at him. That was, until you realized that these hoes wasn't shit and you needed a real one to hold you down.

I sat on the hood of my car while my bro, Project, stood next to me mixing dirty Sprint. I personally didn't fuck with that, but all my niggas stayed indulging. All I needed was a little Hennessy and Crud. Project's cousin, Tyke, was out chillin with us, too, and this nigga had more female drama than a little bit. He sat in his car with the driver's door open with a little chick all in his face questioning him of his whereabouts the night before.

"That nigga crazy out here answering to these bitches." Project said, taking a sip of his concoction. He ain't have a lick of respect for females. In all the years I had known him, I had never heard him say anything respectful about any woman, but I had to agree with him on this one. It was no way in hell I would be wasting energy on the one he was answering to.

"You know ya mans love 'em all and tries to please em' all. I said, laughing loud enough for him to hear me.

"Nigga, you really ain't got much room to talk. Bridgette be all over yo ass. I don't know how y'all do it. I can't find a bitch I like enough to even remember her name." Project said, shaking his head profusely.

"Nah, it ain't that at all. I mean, I fuck with her, but I damn sho ain't in the same boat as that nigga." I said, disagreeing.

"I'm trying to crack Maliah." I admitted.

"Maliah? She pregnant as fuck, by a bitch nigga at that, but she is bad as fuck though." He laughed

Just as he said that, Bridgette's red Mustang pulled up beside us.

"See what the fuck I mean. Y'all niggas are terrible." He said crouched over laughing. "Y'all let these hoes run wild." He added.

Bridgette hopped out the car smiling from ear to ear. I had to tell her too many times about pulling up on me unannounced.

"Hey, Baby." She said walking up to me. I extended my arm to stop her in her tracks.

"What the fuck I tell yo ass about poppin up where I'm at?" She had just killed my vibe, and it was time that I dropped her ass. I had been messing with her for years off and on, because she was the one a nigga could count on no matter what. To say I put her through hell and back was an understatement, but that didn't keep her from still wanting to be by my side.

"Case, you wasn't answering your phone." She said, like that would rationalize the fact that I told her not to pull up on me, ever.

Project was on the sideline still laughing at the both of us like it was the funniest shit that he had even saw.

"Fuck is so funny, PJ?" She asked, cutting her eyes at him.

"Yo silly ass is hilarious." He walked off toward his house with his doubled cup in hand.

I knew him, and he was trying to keep from saying some disrespectful shit to her. Bridgette was still mine, and he knew that I didn't play about shit that was mine.

"Go home, man. I'm not about to talk to you about shit out here." She was a fuckin nag. Every time I looked up, she was, either questioning me about something, or asking me for something, and today I was not feeling any of it.

"Case, you ain't been answering my calls, and yo ass ain't been home in three days, so please let me know when the best time to talk to my boyfriend is?" She huffed.

"Didn't I just say I'm not about to talk to you out here, and why the fuck you got on those little ass shorts and all that makeup?" It was hot as shit out here, and her face was caked up. She knew how bad I hated for her to have a face full of makeup. She was not ugly by a long shot, but her self-esteem was so low, and she was highly insecure in every aspect of her life. That was the main reason it was time for me to let her go. She was too weak of a woman.

"Whatever Case. Can I have some money to get me something to wear to Shawnie's birthday dinner?" Shawnie was my people, and in no way, shape, or form did her and Bridgette mess with one another. She wanted to go so that she could try to keep tabs on me, but it wasn't happening. I wanted to have a genuine good time and not sit around a bunch of females that had a problem with one another.

"You not going to her dinner. I'm about to slide from over here. I will holla at you later." I said getting off the hood. Tyke had left with the girl he was arguing with, and Project was in the house.

She stood the looking dumbfounded, but I wasn't fazed at all. As I walked around her to get in my car, she grabbed me by my arm.

"You got me fucked up; you not about to keep playing me like I'm some sort of lame female that you fuckin with. We've been doing this for too long, Case, for you to still be on this bullshit." Her eyes began to tear up. In all honesty, I wasn't intentionally trying to hurt her, but she knew like I knew that she was no different than me. She probably was worse.

When she was mad or hurt by my actions, I knew she stayed giving that pussy away. I knew that she played that innocent shit, but I was too well-connected to be anyone's fool. For that reason alone, she could never be my Queen. I was a firm believer that any woman that used her body to get back at a nigga or feel better about herself would never be worthy. At least, not in my eyes, anyway.

I continued on to my car; I had business to tend to, and she was slowing me down. I left her standing there to figure things out by herself.

I pulled up on my mama, because it had been a while since I stopped through to see her.

"Where yo black ass been at boy!" She asked hugging me. I had been in hiding for a few days trying to get my mind right, and she hated when I didn't check in with her to let her know that I was good.

"I'm good, Lady; what's been up with you?" I asked, walking toward her kitchen. She always had something in there for a nigga to eat.

"You know ya mama; I've just been hustling." She said, warming me up a plate. She was a true hustla. Everything I knew, I got from her. If I ain't know shit else, I knew how to make a dolla. It wasn't too much that moms ain't have her hands in. Lately, she had been in charge of moving a ton of weight from The Highlands of Columbia to New Jersey. She flew a few nigga's from around the way to New Jersey to break down the product once it crossed the border.

"Yeah, I know; you stay getting to it, but you need to slow it down." I hated the idea of her being in this dirty ass game but she was an OG and addicted to the game. There was no quitting for her, no matter how much I pleaded with her.

"Bridgette came by here looking for you." she said changing the subject. This was the shit that annoyed me the most. She thought that she could pull up wherever. Hearing this added fuel to my fire, and I was so tired of that bitch it wasn't even funny.

"You better stop doing my girl like that; she loves yo crazy ass. You got her running around here stressed out trying to keep up with you." My mama had love for Bridgette, but that was mostly because I kept her out of our business. I wasn't the nigga that ran to her with all of my problems so she stayed in the dark about a lot.

"I'm feeling, Maliah, you remember her?" I asked, finishing up the rest of my food. I couldn't get her face out of my mind. She had a positive spirit on her, and I craved to get close to her. This was the first that I had a desire to get to know a female on a personal level. The relationship

Bridgette and I had just happened without me giving any effort. She didn't make me try hard at all.

"Maliah? Rosie's daughter?" she asked with her nose in the air. I nodded my head yes to let her know that she was right on the money.

"Why her Case?" Disappointment filled her voice.

"Why not her? You know something I don't?" I wasn't feeling her response.

"Well, for starters, she is not your speed. She doesn't have anything to offer you. I just saw her a few months ago, and she was pregnant, and she is so young. I don't understand. It's so many women out there, in which you can have any one of them, and you're sitting here talking to me about her. Not to mention her boyfriend works for us now. I just sent him to Jersey for work." she tried to reason.

The only thing she had said to me that was valid was that her nigga was working for us. That perceived a potential problem. I didn't want to fuck with the money or the process. Another part of me was thinking about the fact that she was pregnant and the nigga was gone. We sent people to Jersey for months to a year. This shit was like going to the military, so I couldn't make logic of him going and leaving her in the gutta with nothing.

"Ma, I'm feeling her, and I gotta at least see what she's about. I don't even know why I'm having this conversation with you," I laughed. Every person that I had come across since I saw her at the diner, I was telling them that I was feeling her. With Bridgette being the exception, I was way out of character with this one.

Her facial expression told me that she wasn't feeling the idea, but I always went against the grain. I saw potential in her, and I was definitely about to see it all the way through.

Chapter 4: Maliah

I called Eriq for the 100th time, and his phone went to voicemail again and again. I decided to call Ayesha, because she was the hood gossiper, and I wanted to see if she'd seen Eriq that day.

"Hello," she huffed into the phone.

"Hey girl; have you seen Eriq today around here? I asked, getting straight to the point of my call.

"Nope, I been at work doing a double all damn day." she said.

"Damn, I ain't talked to his ass today, and he usually texts me all day, but I haven't heard shit." I said frustrated even more.

"He'll call you; he probably been hustling all day; you know how he gets when he's in the streets." she said, easing my mind a little.

"Yea, you're right. Hit me up if you see or hear anything." I told her.

"Will do, Boo." she assured me before we hung up.

I had given Eriq that money, so he was probably out trying to flip it to bring me home something.

That night, I tossed and turned and checked my phone periodically. Light was beginning to peek into the blinds, and I still had not heard from

Eriq. I hadn't slept one bit, and I was beyond tired. I had to call in sick to work, because I couldn't function or think straight. As I flat-ironed Marquita's hair for school, I replayed the last day that I saw Eriq in my head. We were in a good space, we didn't argue or anything, and even if we had, he always checked on the baby and me.

After I got the kids out the house and off to school, my mama came storming into the house. I hadn't seen her in days, and she had scars on her face and arms.

"Ma! What happened to you?!" I asked her examining her face.

"These hoes tried to beat my ass saying I stole from them." she said, lighting a cigarette. All I could do was shake my head in disbelief at her. Looking at her, they didn't try… they did beat her ass.

"Go outside with that smoke." I said, waving my hand in front of my face and fanning the smoke.

"Oh, I forgot about my grandbaby in yo belly." she said going outside. I tried calling Eriq one more time before locking up our room and leaving the house to go pay a visit to where he lived. I couldn't take it at this point. I called him the entire drive to his brother's house, only for his phone to go straight to the voicemail.

When I got to his brother's, I didn't see his car, but that wasn't going to stop me from knocking on the door in search of some answers. If he was hurt or anything like that, I needed to know. I stood on his porch knocking on the door when finally Vanessa, his brother's girlfriend, answered.

"Hi, Vanessa, do you know where Eriq is? I haven't heard from him, and I'm worried." I asked sternly. She opened the door wider and signaled for me to come in.

"Hey, Maliah." she greeted me with her youngest child on her hip.

"Eriq moved out yesterday morning. He took most of his stuff. I assumed he was moving in somewhere with you." she said. I was taken back with what she was telling me. I had to look at her for minute to make sure I heard her correctly.

"He moved out?" I questioned. I had been with him the entire day before, and he didn't mentioned anything about moving out.

"Did he go back to his mama's?" I interrogated her.

"I don't know; I didn't talk to him. Sam told me." she said, sitting the baby down on the couch.

"Where is Sam?" I asked.

"Hold on one sec." She walked toward the back of her house to get his brother . I felt like the wind was knocked out of me, so many thoughts went through my head at once. I was in a state of shock. Sam came from the back of the house with Vanessa in tow.

"Sam, where is Eriq." I wasn't trying to make small talk; I needed answers.

"He moved out yesterday; he said that he had to make some moves, and he needed to go away for a minute." Sam said coolly.

"Did he tell you where he was going?" I was on the verge of tears. Sam looked at me with pity in his eyes and said "No, I don't know where." he lied. I could hear the dishonesty in his voice.

"Sam, I'm about to have a baby in two months, so I need to know where he is and what's a minute? I can't be left hanging like this." I stated with tears now falling freely.

"I know Maliah, but he didn't tell me nothing. He said he would be back, and that was all. I'm sure it won't be long with the baby coming." he lied again. I was wasting my time here. His brother was covering for him, and this shit was foul. Without saying another word, I left. I called his Mama Regina to see if she had seen him.

"Hello?" she answered.

"Hi, Ms. Robinson, this is Maliah. Have you seen Eriq?

"Hi, Maliah! No, Baby. I haven't seen him since yesterday. He came over to eat with me. He seemed a little off, but left shortly after being here." she confessed.

"Okay, if you hear from him, please call me." I pleaded.

"I will, baby. How are you and my grandson doing?" she asked.

"Not okay, Ms. Robinson. I need to talk to Eriq, I need to know he is in this with me." I said more so to myself than to her.

"I will call around to the family and see if they have seen him. If you hear from him, call me. I'm concerned now, too; this isn't like him." she said.

"Thanks, I will talk to you soon." I said to her. I drove around every spot that he chilled at, hustled at, and that I'd ever seen him at, and still nothing. It was like he had fallen off the face of the Earth. The niggas he ran with, I could tell was on the same shit Sam was on. They knew but refused to tell me shit. I felt hurt, betrayed, confused, and scared all in one.

I searched for him and called his phone all day but to no avail. *How could he do this to me?* I thought. I just gave this nigga half of my savings, and he played me. That's how one part of me felt. The other part was feeling like something had happened to him, because there was no way he would leave me and our son knowing my fucked up situation. This couldn't be life.

Chapter 5: Maliah

Three weeks had went by, and I hadn't heard a thing from Eriq. No one knew where he was, and his phone service was now off, so I couldn't leave a voicemail or send a text. I called every hospital, stalked every corner, and there was no sign of him. I had been drowning myself in work and school, trying to stay as stress-free as possible under the circumstances, for my son's sake. I was creeping up on eight months, and I was now solo with my pregnancy.

My mama had seen how distraught I was, and she was making an effort to be there for me. She would come home more and give me shit she found off the streets as a gift. I cried myself to sleep every night. I cried because I missed my man, and the thought of him leaving me stuck to do this alone had me losing my mind.

"Good morning, Lady Bug." my mama said, greeting me as I walked into the kitchen.

"Good morning, mama. " It was Saturday, so the kids were home, and my mama were home. This was unusual on Saturdays; she was always gone before any of us woke up.

"I want to cook you some breakfast." she said. "You cook for us every day; all day. Let Mama feed you." she said, as she began to pull bacon and eggs out the fridge. She hadn't cooked in so long, I was skeptical of eating her cooking.

"Thanks, Mama, but I don't mind; I'll cook." I said.

"No, let me do this for you." she pleaded.

I hadn't had much of an appetite. I was only eating to keep my son healthy. I needed to do something to keep my mind off of what was going on so I called Ayesha to inform her that I would be going to church with her the next morning. I wasn't an overly religious person, but I prayed every day and believed in the higher power. I needed strength, and I knew where to go to get it.

I picked over the breakfast my mama prepared for me and scrolled through my Facebook timeline before noticing that I had an invite from Shawnie to attend her birthday dinner. Shawnie and I were cool. We weren't the best of friends, because I didn't let anyone in to that extent to give anyone a best friend title, but she was always good for a dinner date or a mall run. I was sick of drowning in sorrow and checking my phone every five minutes hoping that Eriq would call me.

My baby shower was supposed to have been last weekend, but I canceled it. I wasn't in the mood to be bombarded with questions or wear a fake smile. All the essentials my baby needed, I purchased on my own, and I received a few gifts from distant relatives.

After contemplating for hours, I decided to go to her dinner. I packed Jaylen an overnight bag to attend a sleepover that he was invited to, then I confirmed with Marquita that she would be home to babysit Kayla while I went out to dinner. It was a damn shame I had to find baby sitters or make arrangements before going anywhere, and my child was not even here yet. Right after my mama cooked, she was out doing what she did best… getting high.

Later that evening, I met the parents of Jaylen's friend to confirm with them what time I would be picking him up the next morning after the sleepover. It made me smile watching him run around with the other little boys his age. I sacrificed my entire youth so that they wouldn't go without or be dirty crack babies that could be added to the statistic reports. These kids were my life, and that hurt me even more to know that Eriq knew how much weight I was carrying and still left me on my ass with three thousand dollars shorter. I pushed that thought to the back of my head and proceeded to the banquet hall for Shawnie's dinner.

When I got there, it was hardly anywhere to park. The place was jumping, and that only made me second guess going in. Crowds bothered me, and I was already irritable from the heartburn that I suffered with throughout my pregnancy. I was here now, so I thought I might as well tell her happy birthday, even if I didn't stay long.

I found a parking spot that was far as hell from the entrance. It took me ten minutes with my slow ass pace to get to the door. I was all belly, and from the back, I didn't look pregnant until I turned around, where you could clearly see I was all baby. My hair was already long prior to getting pregnant, but now it was fuller and reaching my waist line. My breast were fuller, and despite what I was going through, my son had his mama glowing. Dudes were still trying to get on with me, pregnant and all;

they just didn't care. I maneuvered through the crowd until I spotted the table Shawnie was sitting at.

She had not changed a bit since we first met in middle school . She was just taller and sillier than before. Being around her, I was guaranteed to laugh my ass off.

"Heyyy, Baby!" she sang, standing up to hug me. "Look at you, Mama. You still all fine and shit." she said, while rubbing my belly.

"Happy Birthday, Girl." I said, smiling and handing her a card with a gift card inside.

"Thank you; here, you can sit right here." she pointed to an empty chair next to her mama. I hadn't seen them in a while, and it was good to be around genuine people. I spoke to everyone and the server sat a plate in front of me filled with all of my favorites. I was in fat girl heaven.

I felt a pair of eyes staring at me, so I looked around to see if I could match where the sense was coming from. I didn't see anyone staring, so I kept eating and laughing at Shawnie's crazy ass. I sipped my water with lemon, and right as I took a gulp, Case came and sat in the empty chair next to me. I damn near choked on my water surprised that he was there.

"What are you doing here? I asked.

"Well, hello to yo ass, too." he smiled.

"I'm sorry; I didn't mean to be rude, but what you doing here?" I said, resorting back to the question.

"Shawnie is my people. Her mama married my uncle last year." he informed me. I did remember Karen getting married, but I didn't know it was to Case's uncle .

"I wasn't expecting to see you here, either though." he smiled, causing me to smile. I could smell the Gucci Guilty pouring off of him. I felt everyone directing there attention to us at the table, and I assumed that he could tell it made me uncomfortable, because he abruptly stood up to tell everyone bye and left the Hall. I felt a sense of disappointment that he was gone. His presence was everything.

I felt my baby kick hard, bringing me back to the reality that his papa was a rolling stone now. I didn't want to convert to sadness while being there, so I said my goodbyes to everyone, too, so that I could go home and tear stain my pillow. When I got outside, I noticed Case on his phone sitting in his brand new Audi R8 that just so happened to be parked directly next to my car. My Ford Focus looked like a pile of shit next to that shiny, black, sexy ass car. I was hoping he didn't say anything to me since he was on the phone.

"Maliah." he called out to me. *Damn,* I thought.

"What's up?" I asked, looking at him. He looked so perfect hanging out the window eyeballing me from head to toe.

"Come sit and talk to me for a second." I was not about to sit and chat with him. All I wanted to do was go home and cry. He had to have sensed me getting ready to say no, because he got out the car and walked around to open the passenger's side door for me to get in. I stood there for what felt like forever before deciding to get in, and I must admit, my ass felt good against those leather seats. I felt like I was in a spaceship, and he was listening to Future's "March Madness". He turned it down to a whisper after getting back in, then there was an awkward silence before either of us said anything.

"What's going on with you? I can see something is bothering you." he asked. I knew he knew what was wrong with me. Everyone knew I was the talk of the hood about how Eriq left me , and Case knew shit he didn't even want to know about everyone. People just felt a need to report to him with everyone's business. He wasn't getting anything directly out of my mouth, though; no one was.

"I'm cool; I'm tired of carrying my baby. I'm ready to see his face." I perked up saying.

"Yeah, you large out here." he laughed while reaching out and rubbing my belly. No guy had touched my stomach besides Eriq, so when Case touched me, my body froze, time froze, and everything around me froze. I didn't know what was going on, but it felt right; it felt too right. So right that I didn't like it. I politely removed his hand off of me and placed it on his lap.

"My bad; I don't know what made me just do that. I don't go around rubbing on pregnant chick's bellies." he smiled.

"So don't make the exception with me." I snarled. At that moment, I felt like he was sent here to destroy and finish off the little joy I had left in me. I was confused at what had just happened and why did the shit feel like magic.

"Look, it's getting late, and I have church in the morning. I have to go." I said looking at my phone. It was early, not even 8:00 yet, but I had to say something to get the fuck out of his car.

"What church you go to?" he asked me. I know his thug , hustling ass don't care about what church I go to. *He just wants to waste my time.* I thought.

"First Baptist." I mumbled, not wanting to entertain his small talk. I was never a fan of small talk.

"Oh, word? I grew up in that church. I used to have to go every Sunday with my grandma. Pastor Johnson is the truth." he nodded. That shut my negative ass thoughts right up.

"Why don't you go anymore?"

He thought about his answer. "I really don't have an excuse. I haven't been in years and haven't thought about going. Maybe I can go with you soon, and we can pray together." Again, the time froze, and I was feeling that wave all over again.

"Yea, maybe." I managed to utter.

"Well, I don't want to hold you up from your night. I'm going out of town, but I want you to call or text me whenever. I know you have a lot going on, and if I can help in any way, I'm ready and willing." he said, looking at me and sounding like he meant every word.

I unlocked my phone to store his number. I still had a picture of Eriq and me as my screensaver, and my mind was screaming, 'Fuck Eriq,' but my heart was hanging on to the idea of having my little family together and all of this just being some sick joke. I departed from Case, and went home to my Loves.

When I got home, Marquita was running her mouth on her phone, and Kayla was piling gel in her dolls hair. This girl loved to do some hair.

"Hey, Sissy!" Kayla yelled, throwing her doll on the floor and running up to hug me.

"Hey, Princess. Did you have fun with Quita?" I asked her.

"No, she didn't turn on Frozen for me or she didn't let me do her hair." she told.

"Girl, we done watched that movie 200 times today, and I just got my hair done. You not about to play in it." Marquita said, interrupting her phone call. I had to constantly remind her that Kayla was only 6. She would argue with her like they were the same age.

"Well, your hair doesn't look good. I could have did a better job than what you paid for." Kayla said rolling her eyes. I laughed so hard that I felt my baby jump. Kayla was something else, and her smart mouth had no filter. Marquita couldn't help but laugh, too.

"You better get that lil girl before I hurt her." she said to me.

"Come on, Kay Kay, let me give you a bath, so we can get ready to go to church in the morning." I said, motioning for her to follow me to the bathroom.

~~~~~~~~

Church the next morning felt good. It was just what I needed to clear my mind of the events that were taking place in my life. Outside of me fussing at   Jaylen for falling asleep because he was up all night at his sleepover, it was amazing.

I felt like Pastor Johnson was preaching to me directly. I bowed my head and said a silent prayer. When I held my head up and opened my eyes, Case was sitting beside me. I gave him a side eye, and he smiled at me. He was looking handsome in his casual attire. His leather Gucci belt and matching loafers finished off his clean look. *Damn, this is one good looking man.* I thought. He grabbed my hand and bowed his head down to say a quick prayer that sent me into an emotional frenzy. Kayla's observant little self was eyeballing our hands clasp together.

"Who is that, Sissy?" she whispered in my ear while drawing on the church pamphlet. She was very overprotective and jealous of anyone else close to me. Eriq would tease her all the time telling her that he was my favorite person.

"He's nobody." I whispered back to her.

"Then why is he holding your hand?" she questioned. Rather than respond, I held my finger up to my lip and nodded for her to pay attention. I noticed Ayesha's nosey ass looking at us, too, out the corner of her eye. I wasn't uncomfortable around Case, but that was the problem. I was too comfortable with him. I only wanted Eriq. I had been loyal to him since the day I met him, and I hated him for putting me in this fucked up predicament.

Case released my hand and tuned into the message Pastor Johnson was delivering. Service was lit today, and the house was brought down. By the end of it, Jaylen was out snoring, and Kayla was whining that she was hungry. We had rode to church with Ayesha, and she always stayed over speaking to everyone. I made a mental note to take my own car next Sunday. I got her keys from her so I could get in the car, then I put the kids in the car and stood outside to talk to Case for a minute.

"I didn't know you meant so soon with joining me in church." I said.

"Well, I didn't see the need to prolong it. I enjoyed it; I needed the word." he said.

"You look beautiful." he admired me while looking me up and down. I didn't have on anything special. I had worn a white blouse that covered my entire belly, because I hated when pregnant girls wore clothes too small. The skirt hugged my wide hips, and my wedges accented my smooth legs. It was summer, but today it was breezy and the wind had my hair blowing everywhere. I wasn't big on makeup, so my two coats of lip gloss was more than enough for me.

"Thank you; you look okay yourself." I joked.

"I leave for Florida tonight. I'll be gone for a few days." he informed me. I felt some type of way about his announcement. I was kind of getting used to him popping up on me. It kept me on my toes. I snickered at Jaylen and Kayla glued to the window looking out at us.

"They're so big now. I remember them being lil' running behind you." he laughed.

"Yea, they're all grown up now." I said, tapping the glass for them to sit back.

"What's in Florida? Your woman?" I don't know what possessed me to say that. I didn't care why he was going to Florida, or at least, that's what I was telling myself.

"Oh, you're jealous, huh?" he asked laughing.

"Whatever, I was just making conversation." I said nudging his arm.

"Naw, I'm here saying bye to my woman, before I leave. I'm going there on business." he said smoothly.

"I'm not your Woman. I'm taken and you know that." he paused and gave me the yea right look.

"Time will tell." he mumbled. "Can I get a hug before I go?" he asked, holding his arms out. "Come on, it's a church hug. We just finished worshipping together, so you can't say no." he smiled. I leaned in to hug him. Just as we released one another, Ayesha came out the church and was headed our way. She was a heavy-set girl, so it was taking her longer to get to us.

"Ayesha, you had to make sure you got you some dinners before you left." Case said to her laughing. I couldn't help but laugh too.

"Fuck you, Case." she shot back.

"How you go say fuck me in the church parking lot you hypocrite. Ayesha cut her eyes at him.

"You better get out of here before she gives you those hands." I whispered to him laughing.

"I'm going to miss you." he whispered back to me still smiling.

"Bye, Case; safe travels." I said, opening the passenger's door and getting in the car.

Chapter 6: Case

"Case, it's been so long since you've been down here to visit Papi." said Amerena. It had been a while since I had taken a business trip to Miami, but when I was in town, I made it my business to link up with her and her friends. She always knew how to show me a good time. We sat alongside the pool at the COMO Metropolitan hotel.

"Yea, it has been a minute." I agreed, staring at her kiss another girl that was just as bad as she was. I hadn't touched down a good two hours, but I was ready to take on the city for the few days that I was there.

"Let's go." I demanded for the both of them to go toward my room to finish what they were starting, and with no hesitation, they followed my command.

Once we were in the room, the both of them wasted no time coming out of their swimsuits. Their butter cream skin was flawless with not a blemish in sight.

"Te gusta cuando no besamos papi?"

I didn't know what the fuck she had said, but my dick was hard, and I was ready to give it to the both of them. They kept kissing while looking at me out of the corner of their eyes. I didn't want to continue to watch the foreplay, so I grabbed Amerena by her arm and pulled her close to me. She unbuckled my belt and pulled my shorts down. Before I had the chance to step out of them, she placed my dick in her mouth and began to viciously suck. Her friend came over and kneeled down beside her to assist with sucking me off. They had a nigga in heaven.

The next morning, after handling my business and being entertained, I sat on the beach with my boy Dom. He was an older cat that had wise words for every situation you could throw at him. For the most part, when we kicked it, I didn't do much talking. I'd let him school me while I let his words run deep. He had a wife, and together, they had eight kids. I always joked with him saying that, that was why he knew so much; he probably had every scenario possible thrown his way.

"I'm happy you was able to make it here to kick it with an old man." Dom said to me.

"Yea man; it's been a while. I forgot how good it felt this way." I replied.

"So what's new? What have you been into? He asked.

I met Dom over ten years ago, when I was just a teenager. My mom and her husband would bring us down here on their business trips. Dom had worked for them for years with managing real estate properties that they had in Florida. He would often tell me to stay away from the streets. He was well-aware that my parents were in the drug cartel, and he wanted desperately for me to not steer in that direction. I had told him I would try my best to keep out of it, and thus far, I had made good on my promise. My oldest brother went to college to become a chemical engineer, and I ran my own barber shop and car dealership.

My step brothers embraced the game with open arms; it was like my pops had been molding them for it since birth, while my mama wanted the complete opposite for my brother and me.

"Business is good, man; the family is good, and life is good." I smiled, nodding my head and sipping my Corona

"That's good to hear. Speaking of family, when you bringing some babies to come visit me?" he asked, tugging at his beard. His question threw me off guard.

"Babies?" I was trying to get out of a relationship and had just had two females in my room the night before.

"Nah G, it may be a while before that one happens." I hadn't even thought of a future that far out that included kids. That question had me analyzing my entire life. I was now thinking something was wrong with me for overseeing that part of life fully.

"I'm just talking shit; you got a while to think about that. Take it from me, with eight kids, man, I can only dream about the days where I can pick up and go." he chuckled handing me a cigar.

~~~~~~~

Miami had worn me out. After checking out several buildings to open a restaurant there and Amerena and her friend letting me have my way with them, I was drained.

My mind drifted to Maliah. I knew she had to have been stressed with that nigga sliding off on her. I thought to text her in hopes that it would lift her spirits.

Me: Hey, Pretty Lady.

Hours had gone by before I saw that she read my text, according to Imessenger, but decided not to reply.

Her young ass is really not trying to fuck with me. I thought. This was a new feeling to me. Hoes stayed on my phone and in my face, so to have her keep curving me like this was pissing me off. When I made it back to Flint, I made a mental note to pay her a visit.

Chapter 7: Maliah

I was now so close to having my baby boy that I had to go to my doctors' appointments once a week. I was done with the crying, but that didn't take away the hurt or concern. I was tired of popping up over his family's houses hoping to run into him. It was getting to be exhausting at nine months pregnant. I decided to get my hair braided since I was so close to my due date, and I didn't want to deal with my hair being a mess. I went to my stylist Tricey to slay my braids. I hadn't seen her in a while, and after she was done, you were guaranteed to feel like a new woman.

I took Marquita with me for her company. The shop was packed as always, because Tricey was the best stylist in the Flint area. I walked over to the shampoo girl, so she could wash my hair. Marquita had taken a seat close by and pulled out her phone. Tricey had all the gossip about everyone's business. I knew she was sharing mine with others that sat in her chair. Hell, I was hoping she had some gossip on my damn baby daddy's whereabouts.

"Girl, you still ain't heard from Eriq?" she wasted no time quizzing me.

"I have." I lied. I needed to throw her ass for a loop. I knew she thought she had the full scoop.

"Oh, that's good." she said. I'm sure she was now trying piece my life together to herself.

We talked about everything, from who was coming up, to who was losing it all. Actually, I should say that I did the listening and they ran their mouths. I was actively listening when I heard Case's name come up.

"Girl, that nigga got more money than what he know what to do with. He bought Bridgette's ass a hover board and a Birkin Bag for her birthday." One girl said coming from under the dryer to hate. *A hover board,* I thought. Bitches was fuckin for hover boards these days? I snickered to myself.

"That ain't nothing; he bought Kim a whole new wardrobe." Tricey added.

I knew he came with a ton of baggage, in which I was not up to deal with. Especially with all the weight I had on my shoulders.

I had been looking at houses for rent, because I needed to move as soon as possible. Space was so limited in that townhouse that I could not think straight. My mama didn't want to let it go; she loved her cheap rent. That was fine with me if she wanted to stay there, because I honestly didn't want her to live with me anyway. I got tired of having to keep everything under lock and key all the time.

Tricey finished my last braid, and I was too happy because my butt was numb, and I was hungry. She handed me the mirror, and I had seven neat, tight, long, French braids to the back. She had my baby hairs fleeked out. I paid her and gave her a thank you hug. I wasn't coming back with this baby bump. As Marquita and I were leaving, April was coming in with her hair all over her head. For some reason, she looked at me with her nose turned up.

"What's this bitch's problem?" Marquita asked me.

"Who knows, and who the fuck cares." I replied to my sister. She was staring hard and long at us like she had ran into a lifelong enemy.

"This nappy headed hoe is asking to get slapped." I said loud enough for her to hear.

"I need my hair done, because yo baby daddy sweated it out." she said chuckling.

Hearing her say that sent fire through my veins, and without thinking about the well-being of my son or myself, I charged at her, but before I could get to her, Marquita jumped in front of me and hit her with a three-piece combo.

Marquita had some heavy hands, and April's little ass didn't stand a chance. Those blows hit her hard before she hit the ground. All the women in the shop held up their phones and began taking pictures and recording my sister getting down on her ass.

"Come on, Quita; we need to go." I said pulling her. She was still talking shit with a bloody nose and mouth.

"That's why you can't find him, and I'm fuckin him every night." she said spitting blood out her mouth. I wanted to go back and finish her ass off, and Marquita cleaned her ass, but I would have had her spitting teeth out her head. The feeling of my son kicking reminded me that this hoe wasn't worth it, and if what she was saying was true, neither was his bitch ass daddy.

We jumped in my car, and I sped off. When we got home, Marquita was still hype, and I was feeling lower than I had ever felt in my life.

"Maliah, fuck her! The bitch prolly lying anyway." she said rubbing my back.

"That's the point, Quita. Whether she was lying or not, he should have never left me to look foolish in these streets." I cried.

"Man, fuck him, and whoever else has something to say about you. You are the shit. You take care of all of us damn good. We stay clean, you stay clean, and you are a good person. That's what got me going. I hate when bitches have something to say about you. You always keep to yourself and help everyone you can." she assured me.

She was right; if Eriq didn't want to be a part of my life, then that was his lost. If he needed time, all he had to do was tell me, and I would have tried to understand. He left me without a bye, kiss my ass, or nothing. I was sick of worrying about whether he was safe or hurt, while he was out somewhere living off my damn money.

I knew that he was okay, because his family seemed to be okay with him missing. His mama was just as worried as I was, and then after a week of him being gone, she seemed to be at peace. She damn near told me in so many words that she had talked to him. I was over it and him. I went into the bathroom to light my candle and relax my mind in a soothing bath with Jasmine oil. I had finals in the morning, and I wasn't letting anything stop me from successfully passing my classes.

The next day at school, I couldn't get what April said to me out of my mind. What she was saying had to have some truth to it. I had seen her at my job not too long ago, and she was speaking and smiling, but that time, she wanted my head. It was crazy how a side chick had the audacity to be the one mad when they're the one that's messing with your man. I would kill Eriq if he ran off and was somewhere laid up with the next bitch, with my money. While I was carrying his son working, going to school, and raising up my siblings. I really would kill him in cold blood if that were the case.

I tried to push those thoughts to the back of my mind to focus on my exams. After four hours of testing, I was confident that I had done well on my exam. I walked out of school with KFC my mind, when I noticed Case's Audi parked in the school's parking lot. I hadn't talked to him since I saw him at church, and he had been calling, but I blew them off. He wasn't in his car, so I figured he probably was here to see some girl on the campus that he was messing around with, in which I didn't care no way. All I wanted was to get to my chicken.

I spotted my car after walking forever and found Case sitting on top of my trunk with at least two dozen, beautiful, long stem roses in hand. I was floored; I couldn't believe he was here and with a bouquet of flowers that was bigger than I was.

"Yo, this is what I have to do to see you? I have to show up wherever you are?" he asked, hopping off the trunk. He was looking better than ever in a black and red Saint Laurent shirt, red Margiela's, and black jeans. The ice in his ear and wrist were crazy. I had to keep from jumping all over him. Everything about him was solid. Although it was hard as hell, I remained cool.

"You don't have to do anything; you could just leave me alone, you know?" I said, smiling ear to ear, not meaning a word I was saying.

"Won't you come ride with me for the day?" he suggested, ignoring what I said completely. I had no idea why he was so persistent with me. I couldn't offer him a thing. I was still in love with another man, and I came with more baggage than a little bit, yet I couldn't get rid of his fine ass.

"I'm not taking no for an answer; you done hurt my ego enough." he said giving the flowers over to me. Now that I had a closer look, there were three dozen red roses. The bunch was heavy as hell. I had never received flowers before; this was a first for me.

"Thank you; they're beautiful," I said smiling.

"You're welcome; it was my pleasure getting them for you." he said in the gentlest manner. I decided to hang out with him. I had to call Marquita and make sure she would be home with Kayla and Jaylen when they got out of school, and once she confirmed with me that she would, I walked the parking lot with Case.

I felt like the ugly duckling waddling next to a prince, but he always managed to make me laugh when I was with him. He opened the door for me, and it didn't take long before I felt like a Queen with him.

"So how was school today?" he asked, pulling out of the parking spot.

"It was good; I had finals today, and I have a good feeling that I passed.

"That's what's up; I'm proud of you. Don't let nobody throw you off what you're trying to do; especially these washed up bitches."

If I didn't know any better, I would have thought that he was referring to the incident at the shop. I knew, by now, word had probably gotten back to him. Rather than respond, I looked out the window.

"So where we headed to?" he asked.

"I'm riding with you today; it's your show." I replied.

"Oh, is it now?" he asked grinning.

"Not that type of show." I laughed shaking my head.

"I know yo ass is hungry; we about to grab some food."

Now he was talking my language. He ordered a ton of food from the 501 Bar and Grill, and my mouth watered with everything he had them to add to our order. He got it as a carry out.

"So how old are you, Case?" I asked as he drove to pick up our food.

"I just turned 25." he answered.

I knew he was older than me, but not by six years. I wasn't worried about being too young for him, because I wasn't trying to be with him. He was just older than what I would have guessed. I was forty years old in my mind. I had to deal with a teenage girl, a boy going through puberty, and a smart mouth little girl, not to mention a newborn on the way. I was far from being immature.

"What? That's too old for you?" Case asked, breaking me from my thoughts.

"I'm not available so that's not a question for me." I replied.

"Good answer." he laughed. I stayed in the car while he went in to get the food. He came out with two plastic bags full of food, then he sat the warm bags on my lap. I was tight as hell in that seat with my flowers, purse, two bags of food, and a huge stomach. The car was nice, but there was no room for all this shit. He laughed at me trying to get comfortable.

He drove until we arrived at some condos. I assumed that it was where he lived. They were nice, definitely a far cry out from the projects where I lived. He pulled into the garage, and it closed behind us. He grabbed the bags and my purse, as I struggled to get out of the car. It sat low to the ground making it almost impossible for me to climb out. I found myself smiling, as he walked around the car and assisted me on getting out. It was refreshing to know that he was a gentleman, but that didn't stop me from being embarrassed that I couldn't do it alone.

"Where are we?" I asked looking around the empty two-car garage.

"We are home." he said, fumbling through his keys. He finally got the door opened and helped me up the stairs into the kitchen. He sat the food on the counter, and I removed my shoes; my feet had become swollen. Pregnancy had caused everything to become a chore.

The kitchen was clean, and it didn't look like it had ever been in use. Not a dish or stain was anywhere in sight. He opened a cabinet and pulled out one plate.

"You're not eating?" I asked.

"Naw, I actually ate already." he confessed.

"Why the hell you buy me all of this food!?"

He looked me up and down. "I thought that was about right." he laughed. I laughed along with him until I felt the baby kicking.

"You see how he gone play us." I said, looking down at my belly. I caught him staring at me while I was talking to my unborn.

"What type of movies do you like?" Case asked, walking into the living room.

"I like scary movies." I called out looking through the bags of food.

"Nightmare on Elm Street it is." he announced.

I ate my food in the kitchen, while he got the movie started. I had ate so much that I didn't want to move from the bar stool I was sitting on. I felt sleep coming over me, and I knew I wasn't going to make it through the movie.

"Come on; it's about to start." he called out to me.

His living room was cozy. He picked up a remote to turn on the electric fireplace and dim the lights. I joined him on the oversized, comfy sectional and positioned myself to be comfortable. He lifted my legs and sat down before placing them down on his lap. I felt warm and fuzzy inside. This was definitely out of my ordinary. He probably had all the bitches from around the way watching movies up in here. He began to remove my socks and massage my feet, and it felt amazing. I had never had my feet massaged before. All I could do was hold my head back, close my eyes, and pray that he didn't stop.

"Case."

"Yes?" he answered in a low tone.

"What's your real name?"

"Casey... Casey Michael Miller." he said.

"I like that name; I'm going to call you Casey." I told him.

The rest of the evening we asked questions about each other and shared stories about funny incidents that occurred in the hood. It felt good to get my mind away from all that I had going on.

Casey was like the breath of fresh air that I desperately needed. I wasn't trying to take him serious and get my heart shattered again, but he was good for keeping my mind at ease. That night, I slept better than what I had in months. The next day, I had more pep in my step, and I loved it.

Chapter 8: Maliah

"You've been in a good mood lately." Jaylen said, as I stood in the doorway with him and Kayla waiting on the bus to pull up.

"I am in a much better mood, Brotha." I smiled at him. I had been seeing more of Case, and that had caused my mood to shift for the better. He would have flowers sent to me with surprise gift cards to the spa. The effort that he was putting in meant something to me.

The bus came, and I said my goodbyes to Kayla and Jaylen. Just as I was closing the door, a black Suburban stopped in front of my house. A man hopped out of the back seat, then yanked my mama out. I stepped out onto the porch into the brisk air with my pajamas and robe on, as he forcefully pushed her toward our house. She walked up the stairs and was facing me looking a damn fool with pony tails all over head. She always let Kayla put bows and barrettes in her hair. Fear was plastered all over her face. He walked up onto the porch, and I didn't budge from in front of the door.

"Lady Bug, give him some money please." she whispered to me.

"What?" I asked confused. I hadn't had a clue as to what was going on. He pushed passed me and my mama, then slowly walked into the house. She stood there looking dumbfounded.

"What the fuck do you want?" I grimed him.

"Bitch, where is the money?" he snapped on my mama.

"Bitch? Nigga, you better get the fuck up out of here with that." I said, opening the door wide so he could leave. The next thing I knew, he slapped my mother so hard that snot and tears flew from her face. Her frail body crashed into the small coffee table we had.

"You wanna steal from Gino, bitch!!!!?" he roared. He continued to throw blows at her. I ran to the kitchen and grabbed the biggest knife I could find. He had blacked out and was beating my mama. He seemed to have forgotten about me being there.

"Get the fuck off of her!!" I screamed. I stabbed him hard as I could in his shoulder, and I left the knife in him . I was not a violent person, but I had to do something if I wanted to save my mother's life. He stopped in his tracks. My mama laid there unconscious as he sat there in pain. I ran upstairs to grab my phone to call an ambulance. When I came back down, he was struggling to leave my house. He made it outside in the yard, then the driver hopped out to help him in. I closed and locked the door and was now peeking out the window. He was weak and woozy, so I had to have cut an artery in him.

I tended to my mama, but I didn't want to move her, because I didn't know if she was suffering from a concussion. It took the ambulance forever to get there, and when they finally came and carried her out on a stretcher, I was sure that she had lost a lot of blood and that they needed to act quickly. Ayesha had come over, and I told her what happened.

I called Marquita to tell her to go to Ayesha's house after school and wait for the kids there. There was no way I was letting them back into that house. I didn't know what those niggas were capable of doing if they came back. I had to go to the hospital myself, because I felt contractions coming on strong. Brenda, Ayesha's mama, drove me to the hospital. The contractions were coming on so strong that I couldn't worry about the situation that had just transpired. I had to focus on not passing out from the excruciating pain that I was in.

"Just don't stop breathing; we are almost there baby." Ms. Brenda instructed. She got to the hospital in record time, and she parked in the emergency driveway. Shortly after we arrived, I was escorted up to Labor and delivery in a wheelchair. Once I was admitted, and into the triage, it didn't take long for them to whisk me away to the delivery room. It was known that he was coming, but I hadn't dilated enough to start pushing. I refused an epidural, so I was baring the pain with every contraction. I laid there in pain for hours before I heard Marquita's voice. I was so happy to see her when she stood by my side to rub my back like she always did.

"Ayesha has the kids, and mama is in critical care on the second floor here." she informed me. This was a crazy ass day. One that I would never forget.

"How did you get here?" I asked her in between contractions.

"Case brought me. He stopped by the house looking for you." Oh God, I couldn't believe he was there.

"He told me to ask you if you would mind him coming in to see you." she said. I was in so much pain that I didn't care about anything but this being over with. I nodded my head yes to her and bared down for the next strong contraction I was feeling.

Casey walked in with a single, long-stem rose and balloons. I couldn't smile, but my heart did. He was a natural at this. He breathed with me, held the towel in place on my head, and when it was time to push, he held my hand. All the things Eriq should have been doing, Casey was here in his place doing it. After thirty minutes of pushing, at 5:36 pm, I gave birth to a beautiful baby boy that weighed in at 8 lbs. 9 oz. and 27 inches long. I cried like a baby after seeing him.

"You want to cut the umbilical cord, Dad?" the doctor asked Casey. Most guys would have shied away from the idea if it wasn't his son, but he reached for the scissors and cut the cord. Regardless of what I had been through earlier that day and the circumstances against me, my son was worth it.

After holding and admiring him, I had to give him back to the nurses, and before I knew it, I was sleeping.

Chapter 9: Case

I couldn't believe I had just witnessed a baby being born. I was even more shocked that it wasn't my baby being born that I had witnessed. I went by Maliah's house when Ayesha told me what went down. I needed more details on what happened, but I didn't want to ask her right after she had just had a baby.

Whoever it was would have consequences to pay. Her hood was my family's territory, and it was known that everyone was safe unless we said otherwise. I was going to let her rest for now and get to the bottom of the situation later.

I had already been making accommodations for them to stay at my condo, because I wasn't letting her go back there. It was going to be hard explaining to Bridgette's nagging ass who it was that I had living at my condo, but that was another thing that was on my list to deal with later.

I kept telling myself that I was done with her, but she always found a way to make a nigga change his mind. She was submissive and reliable, and for the lifestyle I lived, that was useful to have.

I stood over the hospital baby bed that Baby Aden was sleeping in, and he was perfect. I couldn't understand a man's mindset that would abandon something as precious and pure as a baby.

"How long have you been here?" Maliah asked me, waking up from her sleep.

I had left to go home and shower, so I guess she expected me not to come back, because I made it clear to her that I wouldn't be gone long.

"Not that long; how are you feeling?" I took a seat in the hospital chair next to her bed.

"I'm good; I just can't seem to get enough sleep. My body is drained."

'Yea, I bet; you'll be straight. You just had a baby, so it's going to take you a minute to regain your energy." I reassured her.

Even under the fucked up circumstances, there was no other place I would have rather been. It was something about Maliah that made me drawn to her. I was used to helping my people out and wanting to see everyone doing good, and she was no exception.

I wanted more than to know I could help her; I wanted to call her mine. I knew that I liked her, because women that had kids were not my first pick as my girl, simply because I had a lot of bad experiences with trying to make something work with a few of them. So with her being pregnant, and me sticking around, it was a huge deal in my book.

"I'm craving some Ben and Jerry's Chunky Monkey ice cream." She had a wide smile on her face that caused me to laugh.

"Man, I just told yo ass I was leaving, you could have asked me then." I joked.

"I honestly just woke up with this craving." she said, throwing her hands up to indicate that she was telling the truth.

"Anything else you want, because ain't no more runs today after this one." I said giving in to her.

"Nope, this one is it." she smiled.

"Shit, I thought the cravings stopped after the baby popped out." I said laughing.

I leaned over to give her a kiss before I left the room. I knew that she wasn't going to kiss me, but I enjoyed fucking with her. She knew everything that I did for her was from the bottom of my heart, but I still let it be known that I wanted her.

She gave me this crazy, screwed up face while leaning her head back from mine, causing me to laugh hard.

"You gone be out here defending my kisses one day." I said, still kissing her forehead.

I checked my phone when I got in the car. I had over fifty missed calls from some of everybody. It was Bridgette and my mama mostly that was blowing up my phone.

"What up?" I asked Bridgette's worrisome ass as I was in route to the grocery store for ice cream.

"Case, where have you been?" Bridgette asked calmly into the phone. She had learned a long time ago not to come at me crazy or the conversation wouldn't get far.

"I'm out; why? What's going on?" I knew she didn't want shit but to know my whereabouts.

"I was just on the phone with Brianne, and she told me its pictures of you on Instagram with Maliah and her baby." she said still in a calm tone.

Instantly, I thought about Marquita. She was the only person that had been camera happy in the hospital. I didn't care one way or the other about her seeing the pictures or Brianne's gossiping ass adding her two cents on top.

"You was calling me for that?' I said, not understanding what she was expecting out of the phone call.

"Yea, I am calling for that. Why are you at the hospital with her? I thought she was pregnant by Eriq. It's a possibility that it's yours?

She was annoying me more and more as the conversation continued. I knew that I had to let her go for real and stop playing games with her. I didn't want her in the sense of being my woman, and I damn sure didn't want her questioning me about nothing that I did. I couldn't get mad with her for doing so, because I allowed her to think that that was her position, but now it was up to me to set it all straight.

"Where are you? I want to talk to you about the situation face to face." I was going to let her know what it was before I brought Maliah back to my spot after she was discharged from the hospital.

"I'm at my sister's right now about to leave and go home." she said.

"Alright, I'll meet you at the crib in an hour." I said, before hanging up the phone.

At the grocery store, I searched the ice cream aisle low and high for Maliah's request. I was in deep thought trying to filter through all of the

Ben and Jerry's flavors when I heard a familiar voice a few feet away from me. It was Ayesha and April. *When the fuck did they become cool.* I thought.

I knew that Ayesha was well-aware of the fight that happened at the hair shop with Maliah and Marquita, so I couldn't figure out why they were laughing and being best buddies at the store.

"Yo, where are the kids at?" I asked Ayesha, while mugging April's slut ass. She had been trying to throw it at me for years, but nothing about her was attractive to me so I was smooth on it.

"They at home with my mama." she said, giving me attitude like I was in the wrong for asking her a question.

"Yea, okay." I didn't trust her ass, and I made a note to myself to add her to the list of snakes. Most of those hood bitches were fake as hell. They would talk about each other, then hung each other out to dry left and right.

"Hey Case, yo rude self wasn't go speak?" April asked with her arms crossed and standing in a bow-legged stance.

I looked at her and walked away dismissing her. I wasn't fucking with her before, and I really wasn't fucking with her after that shop incident.

"He so damn rude." Ayesha said shaking her head.

I finally found the ice cream and made my way out of the store.

Now I had to deal with Bridgette. I knew that she wasn't about to take the break up well, but I was prepared to get it over with.

I unlocked the front door to her condo, and when I walked in, the smell of food hit me. She never cooked. I had known her to cook maybe twice the entire time we had been together.

I followed my nose to the kitchen, where Bridgette was standing in her bra and boy shorts going in on the stove. I put the ice cream in the freezer and took a seat in her dining room chair.

"Hey, Baby." she said, walking over to kiss me with a whisk in her hand.

I turned my head for her lips to hit my cheek. I couldn't allow myself to get sidetracked as to why I came here. I could use a good home cooked meal and some pussy, but that would only lead me to be still stuck in this situation.

"I ain't come here for all this, B. You know that I don't want to be here, but you keep trying and settling for a nigga. I gotta be real with you and tell you this ain't where it's at for me." I sat there and waited on her response, because I knew that it was coming heavy.

"What you mean this ain't where it's at for you? You're leaving me for that bitch Maliah?" she assumed.

"I didn't say I was leaving you for anyone. I said I'm leaving, because this isn't where I want to be, and I'm not about to keep playing with you on it." She was about to give me a headache, and I was five seconds from hitting the door.

"So when were you going to tell me you had a baby on the way? You waited for her to have baby to tell me this shit?" She was still making hella assumptions and was now crying crocodile tears. "That bitch is poor and don't have shit Case. She was running around here saying Eriq was her baby daddy, and when the nigga flaked on her, she came running to you, and you too stupid to know it." she said throwing the whisk in the sink.

I was done talking or explaining myself since her ass thought she had the entire situation all figured.

"I had some good news to tell you, but fuck it. Go live a miserable life with her bum ass. You will be back when you see she ain't hitting on shit."

She was talking too much for my liking, and it didn't help that nothing of what she was saying was factual. I didn't care about her news or anything else she had to say. I removed her keys from my key ring and left out. She was screaming all kinds of crazy shit, as I walked down her walkway to my car. When I pulled off to go back to the hospital with Maliah, the only thing that crossed my mind was that I had left her fuckin ice cream at Bridgette's house. *Damn.* I thought. Back to the store I went.

Chapter 10: Maliah

It was time for Aden and I to go home from the hospital, but I had one huge problem… I was not taking my baby back to that townhouse.

My mama was fighting for her life in ICU. She suffered massive trauma to her head, and her body was going into shock from the drug withdrawals. I hated to see her in this condition, but a part of me was praying that this was her wake-up call, and I was going back to Ayesha's place until I could figure out a living arrangement for us.

Casey had only left my side to change his clothes during my entire hospital stay. I gathered our things from the hospital room, while Casey carried Aden's car seat as we left the hospital room. I sat in the wheelchair waiting with Marquita and Aden, as Casey went to get his car.

"I can't believe you brought him here." I said to my sister, referring to Casey.

"Girl, he would have ended up here whether I told him or not, the way he was interrogating people on where you were." she said rolling her eyes.

He was a persistent person so she did have a point. A few minutes later, Casey parked a brand new, shiny, white Cadillac Escalade in front of the hospital.   He hopped out and grabbed Aden's car seat from Marquita, then helped me into the SUV. When we got to Ayesha's house, he instructed Marquita to go in the house to get Kayla and Jaylen. She didn't hesitate to do what he said, but I whipped my head in his direction.

"Why would you send her to get them? I told you we were staying here until I signed the lease on this house." I said giving him attitude.

"You're not staying in this little ass house with all these kids, Maliah, not on my watch."

"Who said I was on your watch? I appreciate you being there for me, but I don't need you to take care of me." I stressed to him.

"You don't have to need me. I just need to know you're straight. Just let me do this one thing for y'all. You'll be comfortable while you take care of your business." he pleaded. I looked out the window, as Jaylen and Kayla were running to the truck. They hadn't seen the baby yet.

"Sissy!!" Kayla squealed.

"Hi, Baby Girl." I said kissing her cheek. They peeked in Aden's car seat and smiled happily.

"He is so cute." Kayla cooed.

"Sit down, y'all, and put on your seatbelts." I said to them, as Casey let the TV down in the back and turned on SpongeBob for Kayla.

"This truck is dope." Jaylen complimented. All five of us, plus Aden's seat fit comfortably.

"Thanks, Bro." Casey responded. After grabbing pizza and wings, we reached our destination, which was his condo.

I was thankful for his help, but I was leery of staying at his place with my family. It was my job to protect them, and although I had known of Casey all my life, I didn't actually know him. He unlocked the doors to let everyone out, but I took my time while he and Marquita unloaded the truck. I made it in the house and was in need of a Tylenol 4.

I sat down on the cozy sectional, as Casey made plates of food for the kids. Marquita took Aden out of his car seat to feed him his bottle.

"I need to talk to yo sister for a minute." Casey said to Marquita. I sat on the couch letting the Tylenol take effect.

"Y'all, can stay here until however long you need to get your place. It's a pull out couch with tons of games for Jay in the basement and three rooms up here.

"You and Aden can take my room, and the other two rooms, the girls can take. I wanna talk to you about the nigga that did that to yo mama. What he look like?" he asked focused in on me. I didn't hesitate to give him answers; I wanted him dead.

"He was tall and heavy-set, with a beard. He yelled out the name Gino. Apparently, my mama stole something from him. It was probably money or drugs" I told him feeling ashamed.

"Gino?" he pondered. "Alright, y'all get comfortable. I'm about to unload y'all stuff and head out." he said standing up.

"Where are you going to stay?" I had gotten so used to his help the past two days that I wasn't feeling the detachment.

"I'm smooth; I have a few places I can stay." he said walking out. I didn't know what that meant, but my inner self was telling me that meant other women to stay with.

"Okay." I replied, looking away. I got the kids settled and comfortable, and I was happy to be back with them. Being away from them was not easy for me. I worried about them every second of the day. They questioned was this our new house, and I had explain to them that we were staying there only temporary.

Later that night, my phone was ringing off the hook. I had finally dozed off after tending to Aden's needs, so needless to say, I was pissed someone was blowing me up. The screen read, and it was Ms. Robinson, Eriq's mama.

"Hello." I huffed into the phone.

"Hi, Maliah; I heard you had the baby. Why haven't you called any of us?" she questioned.

They all knew what I had been going through, and not one of them called to check on me. Hell, if I wasn't blowing them up to see if they talked to Eriq, I wouldn't have spoken with any of them, and they didn't always answer or return my calls then, so this lady really had her nerve.

"Ms. Robinson, I hadn't talked to you a whole month before Aden was born. Throughout my entire pregnancy, I was always the one calling you, so I really didn't see the need to rush to make the announcement to you." I explained.

"Aden? I thought he was going to be a junior?" she asked with an attitude.

The nerve of her to ask me that after I had just expressed my feelings to her. Why in the hell would I name my son after a man that left me right before our baby shower, wasn't there during my delivery, ain't wrote me a Dear John letter, and left us $3000 short? *What stupid bitch would actually do something so dumb?* I thought.

Before I responded to her, I had to say a quick prayer. "Lord, don't let me disrespect this woman. Take control of my tongue." I said to myself silently.

"I liked Aden better, and since Eriq hasn't been seen or heard from it was the first decision I got to make as a single mother ." I explained in which I was done with doing at this point of our conversation. "Look, Ms. Robinson, I'm tired. Once I'm settled and healed, I will bring him to meet his grandmother. In the meantime, I'll send you some pictures. Maybe you can show your son he has a little boy in the world now that looks just like him." And with that, I hung up.

She had rubbed me the wrong way. I had enough to worry about, and I wasn't adding her ass to my list. I rolled back over and plopped my head back down in the oversized, goose-feathered pillow.

Casey's bed was the most comfortable bed I had ever laid down in. His sheets were clean and crisp. The mattress formed to every curve in my body, and I was sure it was like sleeping on a cloud. Aden slept peacefully in his bassinet, while my sisters were sleeping in separate rooms… something that they had never been able to do. Jaylen was in the finished, carpeted basement with every new game console out, a 60-inch HDTV, and snacks galore. He was in pre-teen heaven. I wished this was the life I could provide for them on my own without Casey's help, but the fact of the matter was, we were homeless.

I wasn't taking them back to a blood-stained, tiny, two-bedroom townhouse where crack heads came by every day looking for our mother. All I could think about was I had put them on the bus minutes before that nigga came to our house and attacked our mama. They could have been there and witnessed it. It was no doubt in my mind that, if they were home, I would have slit him from ear to ear, and I would have had a body on me.

I was now off work without pay. My job didn't have benefits, so every day that I was off on maternity leave, it was a day's pay gone. All I had was my savings, and I was using that to get us in a house and a new car. I had to think of something quick, because with four kids, that wasn't enough money to make it for a month. A tap on the door interrupted my thoughts.

"Come in." I whispered. I looked over my shoulder and saw Casey's silhouette. I was happy to see him. After being cooped up with me, I knew he was anxious to get back to his fast life.

"Hey, I wasn't expecting you back tonight." I said in a low tone.

"I missed y'all." he responded. I couldn't see his face, but I could smell him. He always smelled so damn good. He sat at the foot of the bed before peeking into Aden's bassinet. I would have never thought that I would have been sharing these moments with him and not Eriq. It was funny how life worked.

"After collecting my money and tying up loose ends, it felt right to come back here tonight, and I knew yo ass needed some sleep." he chuckled.

He was right about that. After getting Jaylen and Kayla ready for bed and tending to Aden, it made me realize I really had my work cut out.

"Thank you, Casey. Thank you for being here for me. It means a lot to me." I said with gratitude.

"You don't have to thank me, Maliah. You deserve more than this. I admire your strength for real." he said yawning. "I'm about to hit the shower and crash on the couch. The kids need to get back to school tomorrow. I will take them." he confirmed with me.

I didn't want him to take them, but I knew they needed to go, and I didn't want to take Aden out to drop them off across the city for school. I didn't have much of a choice. Ayesha offered to take them, but Casey didn't want a soul to know where his spot was at. He made that clear to us before we all got here, and I had to respect that.

"Okay, I'll have them ready."

He showered in the master bathroom, and I could smell the aroma seeping through the doors with the steam. For the first time since I was with Eriq, I felt horny. Although I couldn't do a thing since I had just had a baby, it didn't stop me from being in the mood. I could feel the puddle forming in between my legs, and I felt dirty, because in my mind, I shouldn't have been feeling like that. I didn't want Casey like that. I clutched my legs together tight and shut my eyes. *I'm going back to sleep.* I thought. Shortly after, the water shut off, and the bathroom door swung open. I should have kept my eyes closed, but no, I had to peek over the covers, and there he was… a black, chocolate Adonis. His chest was chiseled and his biceps were defined. The "V" in his pelvic area was profound and the water dripped down his body leading to the towel he had around his waist to cover the print that looked like an animal was trying to break out of a cage. *Lord't, this ain't what I need.*

Chapter 11: Case

When Maliah told me that the man that attacked her mama yelled out the name Gino, I could had lost my cool right there. Gino was my stepdad. It had been word around the hood that Rosie had stolen an ounce of cocaine from one of his traps and was bragging around the hood about it. Out of respect for Rosie and love for her family, I pulled him aside and talked to him about it. I knew their struggle from watching them since I was a lil nigga, and I knew that, when you had the addiction up against you, your life's decisions weren't always the best.

My stepdad never promised me that she would go untouched, but instead, he shrugged it off like he wasn't upset about the situation. I could not process the fact that he had something to do with Maliah possibly losing her baby, and Rosie losing her life. I could be honest and say that the drug game was not in me, because I carried too much compassion and integrity. In my opinion, women and children were always not to be touched.

I couldn't get to my mama's house fast enough to address the situation. When I got there, no one was at the house. Gino was never there; he had a crib in New York that he was crashing at until the trafficking of the Jersey cartel was complete.

I was not going to call him or my mama to discuss it over the phone, so I waited around until my mama got back home. Waiting for her to get there, I fucked around and went to sleep. The sound of the heavy oakwood front door woke me up. When I walked down the staircase to see her, she had Bridgette with her in tow. The sight of her made my veins twitch. She was like an annoying ass fly that I couldn't get rid of. She had a good relationship with my mama, who couldn't seem to understand the concept of, if I broke up with a female, then so did she.

I hadn't talked to Bridgette since I told her that it was over. She called my phone all day, every day, but every last call went unanswered.

When I made eye contact with her, she immediately looked down. Neither of them was expecting me to be there, and the shock was written all over their faces.

"How long have you been here?" my mama asked breaking the silence.

"A minute, where have y'all been and why?"

"I'm actually getting ready to go, but it was nice seeing you, too, Case." Bridgette placed the bags that she helped my mama to bring in the house and left after giving her a hug.

"You ought to stop treating her so damn bad, Case." my mama said, shaking her head from side to side, while looking out the window at Bridgette get in her car.

"I don't get in your business about the things you do that I don't approve of, so I would 'preciate if you didn't get in mine." I said.

"I need to talk to you about the Rosie incident that I am hearing of." I wanted to get right down to business and not get side-tracked.

"What about her?" she asked nonchalant

"So you know nothing about the attack against her that pops supposedly put out?" I grimed.

"Is that's what's being said? I don't get involved with who he puts hits on Case, and you know it. Why in the hell are you so concerned anyway?"

The lack of compassion was pissing me the fuck off. I had Maliah, her brother, and her sisters living in my house because of an incident that was brought on by my family for a petty ass ounce of coke.

"Bridgette told me you left her because you got a baby by that girl. I've been waiting on you to tell me. WHEN WERE YOU GOING TO TELL ME, CASE!!?? She screamed, bursting out into tears.

What the fuck is going on here? I thought. I was confused on why this conversation had took a whole different turn than what I expected.

"That's exactly why you shouldn't have her ass up under you; I don't have a damn baby, and that's far from the reason I left her. Again, stick to the topic." I snapped.

"I told you I don't know already, and I also told you to stay away from that girl. She's going to cause you more problems than she's worth."

"Alright, if you don't want to talk, I'll go pay pops a visit then to see what's good." I headed toward her front door to leave out.

"Don't do that, Case. You do not need to be going that way. Our family does not need to be traced back toward New York; especially not, because some young bitch has your nose open and you care about her thieving, crack head mama."

Her words sent me into a rage that I couldn't act on, because no matter what, she was my mother. But she was crazy if she thought this would be the end of it.

I had a few other stops to make to get answers. I pulled up on Project to see if he had some answers for me.

"Yo, P, lemme holla at you." I said, motioning for him to leave the crowd that he was with.

He walked over to me with a blunt hanging from his mouth and eyes bloodshot red.

"What's up, nigga? I see you came out of hiding." he said laughing.

"What do you know about the shit that popped off at Maliah's house?"

"Nothing much outside of what Ayesha told me. It sounded fucked up, but I figured it is what it is. It's all about the principle, brotha." he said sparking the blunt and talking a hit.

He was right; it was all about the principle. Had Rosie stolen and not said shit, I believe that my pops would have blown off the situation, but because she was a crack head with loose lips, word was out. If he would have let her get away with it, then he would have had all the crack heads and workers trying him. She had to have been made an example out of. I was fully aware of the code, but that does not mean that I was in agreement with it.

"So what all did Ayesha say went down?"

I knew that he was fuckin her, and that hoes pillow talked. That's what most of them did best.

"Shit really, besides some niggas came through attacked Rosie and Maliah, and that was about it. She mentioned that they were staying with her for a while, but I was just there last night, and they wasn't there. The kids were for a minute at first. I ain't sure where the fuck they are." he admitted.

If I wanted more details it was obvious I had to go to the source. My mama was right; I couldn't go to N.Y. and risk being followed and bringing everyone down, but sooner or later, I was going to get to the bottom of this shit, and when I did, the outcome wouldn't be nice. I had already spoken to leave them untouched, and my requests had been taken as a joke.

Chapter 12: Maliah

I was taking pictures of Aden on his three-month birthday. I put a little Christmas hat on him and an elf onesie, and I snapped away with my phone's camera. He had gotten so chunky since I had him and was always smiling. He had one dimple in his cheek like his dad, low eyes, and a head full of thick, curly hair. He was as adorable as could be, as he smiled at the funny faces I was making at him.

We were still living at Casey's house. I had found a few houses I liked that were a reasonable price, but Casey had a problem with every last one of them. Let him tell it, the plumbing was bad, the landlord was sketchy, the area was too bad, and it was always something. I was to the point where I was going to check them out alone.

He didn't want me to move out, because I was keeping the house clean like it was when we moved in, I cooked every day, and I never asked him for a dime for any of our personal expenses.

I had returned back to work immediately after my six-week checkup, and my classes resumed in January and everything was on track. My mama was discharged from the hospital last month, but it was going to be a slow recovery for her. She was in a rehabilitation center, and I went to visit her every chance I got. She had gained weight, and for the first time in a long time, she looked healthy.

I still had not talked to Eriq, and I wasn't excepting to. I would sometimes wonder if he missed me or wanted to see his son, but I would dismiss the thought before it had a chance to fully play out. If he missed me or wanted to meet Aden, he would have been tried to reach out to me. It was over for between him and I.

There was no coming back from this for him. I still wanted him to be a part of Aden's life, because every child needed both of their parents. All my father was good for was the money he left me after he died, and I didn't want that for my son. He had become attached to Casey, so whenever his little eyes landed on him, his face would light up. That was likewise, because Casey's did, too.

Marquita babysat the kids while I worked the night shift, and occasionally, Casey would stay over late to help me out. He didn't live there with us. I wasn't sure where he was staying, and I didn't question him, because it was none of my business.

Today, Shawnie and I were going to go to the mall. I had gotten my shape back since carrying Aden, and I badly needed new clothes. Ayesha was watching the kids, and Marquita was going to the movies with a boy named Josh that she had been dating. As soon as she told me she liked a boy, I had her go down to the clinic for the free birth control pills and condoms they gave out. She swore that she wouldn't doing anything, but I was not taking any chances. Life was hard enough for us, and I was not having it.

It was good seeing Shawnie, so I hugged her tightly when I first laid eyes on her.

"Dang, girl! Yo snap back game is strong." she laughed admiring my shape.

I had on a fitted satin Detroit Pistons jacket, Seven skinny jeans that hugged my round ass and wide hips tight, and a pair red Hunter rain boots that were perfect for the rain and snow mixture we had gotten the day before. I loved going to the mall this time of year with all of the Christmas decorations up and sales in every store. I was in a happy place in life where I felt like it could only get better. I laughed at Shawnie's comment.

"You look good yourself." I said to her.

We walked the mall laughing and reminiscing. I bought the kids some clothes and Christmas gifts, and I bought myself a few things I wanted. Casey crossed my mind, too; wanted to buy him something, but I didn't have a clue as to what to buy him. I didn't have that much money, and he had everything. I wanted to give him something to say thank you for all that he had done for me. He didn't ask me for money or pressure me for sex, and he was a gentlemen whenever he approached me.

My phone vibrated in my jacket pocket, and it was him calling. A smile spread across my face.

"I was just thinking about you." I chimed into the phone.

"Is that right? What were you thinking about?" he asked.

I don't know what made me say that to him. I thought.

"I'm just Christmas shopping." I said, wiping the smile off my face. I didn't want him getting the wrong idea.

"Christmas shopping?" he said sounding disgusted.

"Yea, I wanted to get you something thoughtful." I replied to him.

"That's a nice gesture, but I don't need anything. Is that where you are? Out Christmas shopping?" he asked.

"Yea, I'm at the mall with Shawnie."

"Where are the kids?"

"They're over Ayesha's and Marquita is at the movies." I left out the date part, because he had become a little overprotective these days.

"Call Ayesha, and tell her I'm about to come and get them." he demanded.

"Casey, they've only been there for two hours." I huffed. He acted like they were his kids. I was responsible for them, not him.

"Two hours is a long time. Tell her I'm on my way." Before I could say anything else, my phone informed me that the call had ended.

Whose daddy does this nigga think he is?

As I was calling Ayesha, Shawnie stepped out of the fitting room modeling a cat suit that I could never be bold enough to wear. I gave her the thumbs up, though, because it fit her body well.

"Hello." Ayesha answered.

"Hey, girl. Casey is on his way to pick the kids up." I told her.

"Yea, I know. He's here already." she said seemingly annoyed. She had missed us, and she already had strongly expressed to me how she felt that he was taking us away from her.

"We will be with you all day on Sunday for church." I assured her.

"Okay, cool." That seemed to cheer her up as we said our goodbyes.

Shawnie and I stopped at the food court to get a bite to eat before we called it a wrap.

"So what's been going on with you and Case?" she asked, stabbing at her salad. I knew this question was coming.

"Nothing really. He's been helping me since Eriq's ass flaked on me." I shrugged.

"Nothing? You ain't doing nothing with that?" she fumed.

"Girl, you is crazy. Case is the man of the year around here, and you got him at your fingertips. We had a dinner at my mom's house for his grandma, and Bridgette's ugly ass was there, but he wasn't feeling her. He kept his distance from her and was showing us pictures of Aden's cute self."

My heart dropped hearing that he was in the same vicinity as Bridgette. I knew he was seeing other people, but to hear it being confirmed from a reliable source was a tough pill to swallow.

"Yea, him and Aden are two peas in a pod." I said, with a smile to try and mask the hint of hurt I was feeling.

"I mean, he wants you, so why not at least give it a try?"

"I've just been hurt bad, Shawnie. You know better than anyone how much I love-...loved Eriq. I'm still broken, and I don't want to be on the next thing popping, and I'm still hurt." I opened up.

"That's so understandable girl, but you know God works in mysterious ways. Sometimes, one door has to close so that another one can open." I let her words soak in as we finished our lunch, before we headed towards the exit.

"Speaking of the devil." Shawnie mumbled. I looked over to see who she was referring to and spotted Bridgette and her sister staring at us.

"Hey, Shawnie!" Bridgette spoke dramatically.

"Hey." Shawnie spoke back nonchalantly.

"I wasn't expecting to see you here." she said swinging her long weave.

"I was actually just leaving." Shawnie said turning back to me.

I knew that Bridgette knew who I was. She probably knew something about every person that Case had ever spoken to in his life. By looking at her, she didn't look like she would be his type. She was so made up, but I could tell that underneath it all, she was not cute.

"Girl, I don't blame you; it's packed in here. I just ran up here to grab something to wear for tonight. Case and I are going out." she had to add that in there, and all I could do was shake my head. She looked at me like I was crazy for shaking my head.

"Well, have fun." Shawnie said blandly.

"We will." Bridgette said, looking directly at me.

"I'm Maliah; I don't think we have ever met." I said to her since she had problems with her eyes. I hated messy bitches I never came for any of these hoes, yet they stayed in my face over a nigga.

"I know who you are. My boyfriend is helping your family out. Aren't you like homeless or something?" she smirked.

I wanted to punch her dead in the face, but I was now a mother, and I wasn't going to resort to violence unless someone wanted to square up, because I wasn't running from anyone.

"Actually, I'm not homeless. I live in Casey's condo. The condo that he doesn't want me to move out of." I said with my "now what bitch" face.

I could see the hurt all over her as she scrambled for a comeback, but I didn't give her the satisfaction. I walked away from the salty bitch with grace.

When I got to Casey's house, they were in the living room watching Home Alone.

That was my all-time favorite Christmas movie. Aden was knocked out sleep with his mouth wide open, laying on top of his blanket on the couch. Casey was sitting beside him with a longneck Corona in hand. Kayla was laid out on the floor in front of the fireplace, wrapped up in her frozen blanket, and Jaylen was right next to her with his eyes glued to the TV screen. The view was picture perfect. I snuck the bags down to the basement storage closet, and when I turned to leave out the closet, Casey was standing there, and he scared the shit out of me.

"You left Aden on the couch unattended?" I panicked. He screwed up his face.

"Naw, I didn't leave him unattended. I put him in his bed." he said, sounding offended. I was upset with him. The only way Bridgette would have known that I was homeless was him telling the bitch my business.

"Are you all finished with your Christmas shopping?" he asked.

"Yea, I'm finished. Casey, I found a house that I like, and I'm going to put my deposit down on Saturday." I refused to be someone's charity case, especially to a person that I didn't ask for shit from.

"What house? I told you that house had a bad roof." he said, with a vein jumping in his neck.

"Not that house. I went and saw one I liked on Monday before work." I said, walking away from him. He grabbed my arm gently and pulled me back to him.

"Why would you go look at a house without me?"

"I don't have to look at houses with you Casey. Once I move out of here, we will remain friends, but that's all." I said. I could see the stress overcome his body.   "Look Casey, you know I've been through a lot.

I'm still going through a lot, and I don't need to worry about a relationship."

"I'm not asking you to worry at all, and I've been here showing you that you don't have to go through shit alone. I'm here." he said standing in front of me.

"I don't need you to be here, and I don't appreciate you sharing my business with your bitch." I spat.

"What? You got me all the way fucked up. I don't share business or whatever the fuck you're talking about." he said.

"Right, so that's why Bridgette was in my face saying I'm homeless?"

"Man, I tell you all the time, stop sharing yo business with these hoes. They all talk, and I tell Marquita the same shit. I didn't tell her shit about you. The streets talk. Hell, you talk, and you ain't fuckin homeless!" he yelled angrily.

I hadn't seen him pissed off before, and I honestly didn't want to again after just witnessing it. He was always nice and gentle with me, and I wanted to keep it that way.

"Look, fuck all that stupid shit you talking about. You ain't moving nowhere until I see it first." he said dismissing me.

"You can't tell me what I'm doing. You have a girlfriend. Aren't y'all going on a date tonight? You are not my man, and I'm getting the fuck on." I said, rolling my eyes and snaking my neck.

"Yea, whatever." he said walking away from me. He really thought he could tell me what to do. I knew moving here was a bad idea. This nigga was holding me hostage. After the kids were in bed, and Marquita had gotten home, I could finally unwind.

I watched Casey getting ready to go on his date with Bridgette. I pretended like I didn't care, but I was heated on the inside. He wore Balmain jeans, navy Balenciaga's, and a cream-colored sweater. The diamonds he wore accented his outfit. His hair was freshly cut, and he smelled heavenly. I was having the hardest time pretending like my phone had my undivided attention. Aden was in his crib sleeping, because he had outgrown that bassinet with the quickness.

It was killing me, because I didn't want him to leave. He got dressed like this all the time, but because I knew he was going out with her, I couldn't take it. I was a jealous woman right now. I had to be real with myself, these past five months I was falling deeper and deeper for Casey. I spent every single day around him. He did more for me than anyone in my entire life had ever done, and he was a sexy ass man. How could I not feel something for him? I had to resort to drastic measures to try to persuade him to stay. I rushed into the bathroom after grabbing a camisole tank top and a pair of shorts. I mean, ass falling out the bottom, short, spandex shorts.

As he was on the phone in the kitchen, I changed out of my usual old lady pajamas and put the skimpy clothes on. I had cleavage for days, a flat stomach, and a nice ass. I grabbed the coconut oil from under the sink and oiled myself down, before spraying perfume on my wrist. I let my hair fall out of my bun and down my back. I was naturally sexy, but giving him a little more to think about would hopefully do the trick.

I wasn't trying to get fucked, but the way he was looking, putting up a fight would have been a losing battle for me tonight. I came out of the bathroom, and he was still in the kitchen on the phone, which was perfect for my plan. I went into the kitchen to prepare bottles for Aden. I walked past Casey, and I could sense his eyes plastered on my every move. He was giving his phone conversation little interest.

"Aye, nigga, I'm going to hit you up tomorrow about that." he said ending the phone call.

"Why you got that little shit on?" he asked, with lust-filled eyes roaming my body.

"Boy, I'm about to prep Aden's bottles and go to bed." I said, silently praying he would keep engaging with me.

I didn't like playing this game, but I pushed him away so many times that this was the only logical thing to do in my head. He was used to females throwing themselves at him, so I wanted him to continue to pursue me. I hadn't had any sexual encounters going on in months, and my hormones had been raging this past week.

"You must want me to put your flame out." he smiled.

"What?" I asked pretending to be confused. *How was he going to flip this on me?*

He walked over to me and removed Aden's bottle from my hand. He was so close I could smell the hint of Hennessy on his breath. My breathing got slower, and he leaned down to kiss me. His kiss was passionate and deep, while he held my head steady as he assaulted my mouth. When he broke the kiss, I was left trying to catch my breath. My pussy was wet, and my heart was pounding.

"Ask me to stay home and please you." he whispered in my ear with my back pinned against the cold, stainless steel refrigerator.

I looked him in his eyes high off his kiss. I didn't want the words to come out of my mouth, but my body was against it. I was scared. I didn't know how I ended up here. I was supposed to have been with Eriq. *Whose plan was this?* I thought.

"I want you to stay home." I said to him meaning every word.

"Why do you want me to stay?"

"To please me." I said boldly.

I couldn't hide it or pretend any longer. He kissed me again and ushered for me to go into the basement. The house was quiet, because the kids were all sleeping. Jaylen had fell asleep in Kayla's room.

The only sounds being heard was me kissing him. It was like I had found my new favorite thing to do. Kissing him was therapeutic to me. I had gotten lost in his kisses as I sat down on the couch, and he kneeled down in front of me on the floor. It was dark so I was unsure of what was getting ready to happen. He placed soft kisses on my inner thighs and brought his head down in between my legs so that he was up close with my most prized possession. I lifted my hips for him to remove my shorts. He then removed my tank top freeing my breast. I was now completely naked and felt like I was on the verge of having an anxiety attack. No one had ever touched me sexually but Eriq. The anxiety went out the window as he dived in face first to devour me. I wanted to scream at the top of my lungs, but I knew I would wake the entire house up. I had to scream in silence.

The way he ate me had surpassed anything I had ever felt. The way he applied pressure to my throbbing clit had me ready to explode at any minute, and it wasn't long before I did. I laid on the couch paralyzed. I heard him stripping down piece by piece. It felt like everything was happening in slow motion, but that was just me wanting to savor the moment. He laid his body over mine, and I just knew I had died and went to heaven feeling his naked body lying on top of mine. He pushed my legs back.

"Put it in." he said in a low, husky tone. I reached my hand down to grab it and hurried to release it. He was going to split me in two with this weapon. I didn't want him to think I was being childish, so I attempted to put it in. I was leaking down there, but it was still like trying to force a nail in a wall, and the only thing to do was to hammer it. I was nervous as shit.

He took his two fingers and eased them into me, and it felt so good. I was grinding my hips and fuckin those fingers. As I relaxed and grinded my hips more, he began to kiss on my neck. Before I knew it, he had removed his fingers and rammed his thick dick inside of me. Upon entry, he placed his hand over my mouth to drown my howl. This nigga was a professional dick slayer. It was tight, but once he got a good rhythm, it began to feel too damn good. He suckled on my nipples, as he rocked me back and forth. My breasts still had milk in them, but he didn't seem to care at all about that. I came over and over again on him, and I had his pelvic area wet up. His sex was stalker good. I wrapped my legs around him in fear that he was going to disappear somewhere.

"You feel so good, Maliah." he said in my ear. Hearing him say my name caused another down pour.

I had died a hundred deaths that night. We had sex until Aden started to cry , but by then, we had both gotten off numerous times. I staggered to the dryer for a clean towel to wrap my body in. I couldn't feel my legs, but I managed to make it up the stairs and into the kitchen to warm him up a bottle. When I got to the room, he was fussing something serious.

"Okay, Man. I'm here." I said, picking him up and holding him in my arms to feed him.

He was halfway through the bottle when Casey walked in. He had his clothes back on, but when he got into the room, he closed the door and stripped down to his briefs and socks. He got in the bed next to me and under the covers. This was the first time he had gotten in the bed since I had been here. After burping Aden, I laid him back down. I dropped the towel to the floor and climbed in bed with Casey. He moved his body into mine and rested his head in the crook of my neck.

"Maliah." he called out to me with sleep consuming his voice.

"Yes, Casey?"

"You are mine. You and these kids are mine now. Don't forget that."

I didn't want to be any place else but where I was. I was done putting up a fight. This was put together by something that was far beyond my control. It felt destined to be right here with him.

Chapter 13: Maliah

Christmas morning was here when I heard Jaylen and Kayla running to the living room. I climbed out of bed and checked on Aden. He had been fussy all night, and he was finally sleeping.

"Casey, wake up. The kids are up." He opened one eye and slowly got out of bed.

We went into the bathroom to handle our hygiene, and he followed me out into the living room. The kids went crazy opening all of their gifts. I had bought them a few things, and Casey acted as if he was Santa Clause himself. He went all out for them.

Marquita finally decided to join us in opening the gifts. She had been in real teenager mode with a moody attitude. Jaylen had three pair of Jordan's, Nike jogging sets, a gamer chair, a hover board, Nerf guns, and he was still opening.

Kayla had a doll house that was taller than she was, Barbie's mini salon and a stainless steel kitchen set, but and she stopped opening after the salon. She was so excited; doing hair was her thing. She was giving all of her dolls a makeover.

Marquita had The North Face jackets in every color, an iPad mini, iTunes gift cards, Gucci rain boots, and a Gucci wallet with $1,000 in it. He had set the kids up nice. Their faces lit up, and seeing them yell thank you to us with gratitude made life worth living. That was what they deserved and that was the best Christmas we had ever had.

"Thank you." I mouthed to Casey from across the room. He didn't respond; instead, he went behind the tree and came from behind it with a stack of boxes for me. I was shocked, because we agreed on no gifts for each other. I took a seat next to the stack of boxes and began unwrapping each gift.

When I was finished, I was the owner of an Alexander McQueen bag, three-carat diamond earrings, Chanel perfume, and a Canada Goose Montebello Parka coat. These items combined was more than everything I owned.

"Thank you!" I said kissing him and forgetting that the kids were in the room.

They all looked at us in bewilderment. Marquita knew we had become closer than usual the past few weeks, but kissing took them all by surprise.

"Ewww." Kayla said breaking the ice, and we all fell out laughing.

I whispered to him. "I have something for you too." He followed my lead to our bedroom. He closed the door and locked it behind him.

"You need to chill; it's not that type of gift." I said laughing. His freak ass was always ready. I went into the nightstand for the gift-wrapped box.

"We said no gifts, Maliah."

"What?! You got your nerve after all that shit you bought." I said laughing.

He tore the wrapping off and opened the box. There sat an engraved Chronograph Bulova watch. It wasn't flossy like his Rolexes, but I paid a pretty penny for it.

"This is nice, Bae." he said examining the watch. Inside the watch, it read "Frozen in time". He pulled me into him for a kiss, and right when we were into it, Aden started crying. We laughed, because he was right on queue.

"Man, you gotta stop blocking like this." Casey said to Aden.

We visited my mama for Christmas at the rehabilitation center, then we all rode together with Casey to drop gifts off at his mama's house, and she had a house full of people. His mom was a real estate agent like him from my understanding, and they owned several rental properties throughout the surrounding areas. She had been in the business for the last fifteen years, and she owned a bakery in Downtown Detroit. Casey had come from a structured family; his upbringing was complete opposite of mine.

I helped Kayla out of the truck, and Jaylen hopped out on his own. Marquita went to hang out with her friends at a Christmas party. She ditched us every chance she got. Casey carried Aden's car seat as we all walked into the house together. This was my first Christmas spent around anyone else outside of our household.

"Hey, Baby!!" an older woman said grabbing Casey up. She was clearly drunk, and he was cautious not to drop the car seat as she squeezed him to death.

"Hey, Auntie." he said hugging her back with his free arm.

"Auntie, this is my girl Maliah, her brother, Jaylen, and little sister, Kayla. We all politely spoke to her. He made his rounds introducing us to everyone that was important to him, and I had never held a conversation with his mom before, but she and my mama were acquaintances when I was younger before my mama got heavy into drugs.

"Casey, yo ass is always late." his mama said hugging him.

"Merry Christmas, Mama. Do you remember Maliah?" he asked her.

"How can I forget her pretty self?" she said to him uneasy. The way she said it seemed sarcastic to me, but I chose not to give it any thought.

"Give me a hug, and these are the kids? Ooowww, look how big they are!" she said hugging me and the kids.

Casey went into an office that was adjacent to the room we were in to take the baby out of his car seat and snow suit. He came back into the room holding a wide-eyed, bushy-tailed Aden . He looked around the room, and his bottom lip trembled before he started crying.

"Aww, he don't know y'all." Mrs. Rice, Casey's mama said, reaching out to hold him.

"He don't know you either." Casey said laughing. As soon as she touched him, he went crazy on her. Casey had to take him back.

"Y'all got him rotten." she said, gladly giving him back.

We mingled and ate with his family, and it felt so nice to be around genuine people on the holiday. My heart was full and I was thankful Casey allowed me to experience this moment with his family.

We were finally home, and I couldn't wait to lay up in his arms.

"This Christmas was everything. I appreciate you sharing it with us."

"Thank you for allowing me to do it." He kissed my forehead and was sleep before I could say anything else.

I said a silent prayer that this feeling would never end and joined him.

BUZZ!

I woke up in the middle of the night to Casey's phone vibrating on the dresser. It had been ringing non-stop, and it was starting to piss me off.

"Casey, wake up and see who that is." I said pushing his arm. He rolled over so that his back was now facing me.

"I don't care who it is." he groaned.

"It's waking me up; at least turn it off." I complained.

"Then, turn it off Maliah."

He had one too many drinks that night, and I knew that I was making him mad by waking him up. I slid out of the bed to turn his phone off, because I had to get sleep when I could. Aden was still waking up in the middle of the night.

When I picked up his phone to power it off, there were over fifteen missed calls from Bridgette displaying on his phone. I never asked him about their relationship after we began to get serious, because he came home every night, and I had no reason to be insecure.

I now had all negative thoughts consuming my mind after seeing how many times she had called him during the night. I powered the phone off and got back in bed. I laid there debating on if I should confront him about it. I wanted to do more than confront him; I wanted to take that phone and launch it at his head. Going against my better judgment, I decided to lay there in my feelings until the sun came up.

Chapter 14: Case

"WHY IN THE FUCK DO YOU KEEP CALLING ME?" I yelled into my phone.

Bridgette kept blowing my phone up telling me that she was pregnant. I had no reason to believe it was by me. I hadn't been fucking her recently, and word was out that she was out there big as hell. If her dates were correct, there was a chance that I could be the father, but I wasn't entertaining the idea until I had a blood test.

"Case, I wanted to tell you that we are having a girl. It's a damn shame I have to call you 100 times just to give to you updates about your baby." she said huffing.

"I told you to call me when you went into labor. Until then, I'm not fuckin with you, and you are going to get yo feelings hurt if you keep calling my phone."

I was tired of her shit. The more I analyzed our past relationship, the more I realized that she was always more headaches than what she was actually worth. I wasted so much of my life staying with her for all of the wrong reasons.

"My feelings hurt Case? You have ran my feelings over. I don't have any more feelings. I'm going through a pregnancy alone."

If the baby was mine, I wanted to be more supportive, but with me knowing the way she was cut, there was no way in hell I would be out here like a sucka. I already had a ton of stress on me just off of the possibility of it being mine. I knew that it would put a hurting on my relationship with Maliah, on top of me not wanting to deal with Bridgette for the rest of my life.

"It breaks my heart that I am pregnant with your child and you are leaving me on my own, yet you take of a kid willingly that ain't yours." she cried.

She had struck a nerve in me.

"I never said I wouldn't support my baby if she's mine, but until I can prove it, stop calling my muthafuckin phone." I ended the call and blocked her number.

I sat in silence in my car for a while letting all of my thoughts run free. I was dealing with a lot. I loved Maliah and wanted nothing more than to make her happy, but I was still battling being a one woman man as well as getting used to the idea of being a family man.

I decided to go to the bar to get my mind away for a minute. I was sure that a few drinks would do the trick.

When I got to the bar, there wasn't a lot of people there, just the way I liked it. I was not a fan of huge crowds, especially when alcohol was involved. I tucked my pistol on my waist and got out my car to go in. The inside housed its usual customers, and I had been a regular since I was old enough to drink.

"Case, my man!" the owner yelled out to me from behind the bar.

"What's going on man?" I asked embracing him with a handshake.

"The usual man, maintaining. You know how it goes."

"I feel you; that's all that's left to do. Po' me up a double shot of Henny."

As I chopped it up with Eddie, this square ass nigga came and sat directly next to me. I purposely looked up and down the row of empty stools. It was plenty of room, so he ain't have to sit up under me.

"How is it going Casey?"

As soon as the words escaped his mouth, I knew that he was an informant, and now the question held why the fuck was he barking up my tree.

I looked him up and down with menacing eyes.

"Who the fuck are you?"

"I'm officer Gerald Adams; nice to meet you." he said holding his hand out to shake mine.

I left his hand extended refusing to shake it.

"I'm only here to ask you a few questions," he said.

"I ain't got no answers for you." I took my drink from Eddie's hand and threw it back.

"At least hear the questions before you go telling me that you don't have any answers. Do you know a Rosemary?"

"Naw, I don't know a Rosemary."

I was going to call my lawyer as soon as I left the bar. I had no idea why was he sitting there questioning about Rosie, and I wasn't about to ask him questions on why was he there.

He began to lay three pictures of her down on the bar. I examined the pictures of her being beaten so badly that I did not recognize her. The pictures made me even more upset that my dad had something to do with this.

"She said it was your family that did this to her, and I want to know why." he said, picking the pictures back up off the table.

"I don't have any answers for you."

Eddie sat the glass of beer down in front of me, and I wasted no time drinking it down.

"Well, I know that you're not going around beating junkies down this brutally unless drugs are involved. How are your mama and brothers? You think that they have some information for me?"

His questions would remain rhetorical, because I wasn't saying shit else to him about the situation other than what I had already stated.

"Are you finished here?"

I placed a fifty dollar bill on the bar and left him sitting there.

I had to go talk to mama about what had just happened. The last thing that we needed was to have police snooping around over Rosie during the biggest drug trade of our family's legacy.

"FUCK!" I yelled, hitting my steering wheel.

I hadn't done a thing to Rosie but try to help her over the years. She was well-aware that it was my pops' spot that she had stolen from. Once the police started asking her questions, I knew that she would get to singing. A crack head had no loyalty, and I understood why she had to be killed. She had made herself a dangerous liability over a petty ass ounce.

As much as I had tried to lookout for Rosie by keeping money in her pocket, and refusing her drugs, it didn't mean shit to her. Anytime I would see her at one of our traps, I would tell our team to never serve her. I was guessing that's what drove her to steal from us in the first place. She would often tell me how she hated going to the other side of town to cop her product.

The fact that my entire family could go down for this shit had me wanting to go kill her right then and there. She wasn't a blessing to Maliah, anyway. It was because of her that they went through all of the struggles they faced.

I placed a call to my lawyer and paid my mama a visit. As bad as I didn't want it to go down like this, Rosie had to die.

Chapter 15: Maliah

Today was my 19th birthday, and when I woke up, the house was quiet, which was very unusual. Our house was always jumping when everyone was home. The kids were at school, but Aden would be loud and demanding a bottle at this time of the morning. I walked through our condo, and there was no sign of Casey or Aden.

"Bae!!" I yelled down the basement stairs. Nothing.

It was now May. The sun was shining, and the birds were chirping. Casey and I were still going strong. We had a few disagreements here and there and a few hoes tested me, but for the most part, we were good. We started looking at houses, because the condo wasn't holding all of us anymore.

Aden was now eight months old, and we needed him out of the room with us. I quit my job at Chicken Shack, because I had gotten sick of Casey complaining about me working there, so I followed through on an offer as a secretary at an attorney's office. I was going to school to become a criminal defense lawyer so it was beneficial for me to gain some knowledge and get paid while doing it.

Casey didn't believe in me helping to pay the bills. He said it was his job to provide for us. It bothered me that he felt that way, because I was so used to being independent. I didn't have to buy much with my money, because we had everything we needed, so I saved the majority of it.

My mama was released from the rehabilitation center last week and was already right back to her same ways. After having to relearn how to take care of herself all over again, you would have thought that she would have been done with the streets.

She remembered the attack vividly, because I talked to her about it a few times, and she had given me several different names on who had attacked her. Case was one of the names she mentioned, and then turned around and said another man's name. The doctor told me that her memory was not reliable, and that she would likely continue to give off the names of people who she knew well. I prayed that she would change her ways, but for some reason, she just didn't want that for herself, and I was slowly learning to accept that.

I called Casey to see where he and Aden were.

"Happy Birthday!" he shouted into the phone.

"Good morning, Baby. Thanks, where are you?"

"Getting ready to pull up on you. I wanted to grab our birthday girl some breakfast. Open the garage door."

"Okay." I hung up the phone and opened the garage door. Seconds later, Casey pulled into the garage in a new Cadillac ELR Coupe with a bow on it.

"Oh my, God! No he didn't!" I screamed to myself as I jumped up and down in our kitchen. With no shoes on, I ran into the garage and around the car. "You didn't! Thank you so much!" I cried.

He got out the car and handed me the alarm pad. I could not believe this was my car. No more Ford Focus for me. This car was the shit, and it was all mine. I planted a thousand kisses on his face before I climbed in the back seat with Aden.

"This is our new car, Baby?" Aden smiled at me like he knew what I was saying. I unstrapped him out the car seat.

"Now you have an ELR and the Escalade." Casey smiled. He always drove his R8 or his Challenger. He only drove the Escalade when we all were going out together. He would always say the Escalade was mine, but because he had it before we got serious, I never viewed it as actually being mine.

I walked back in the house with Aden on my hip, and I was the happiest woman in the world. I was living the life that I had prayed for. I sat Aden in his high chair and poured Cheerios on it for him to snack on. Instead of eating the cereal, he decided to launch it across the kitchen, as Casey walked in the house with breakfast.

"We are going out to celebrate tonight." he informed me.

I hadn't had a night out since my 18th birthday, and I was pregnant then.

"For real? Are we going out like turning up or like dinner?" I didn't care whichever one we did. Hell, I was happy to be getting out the house.

"Both. My mama gone watch the kids. I doubt if Marquita will be home." he said, taking a bite of pancakes out of the Styrofoam container.

Marquita had been coming home less and less lately. She was seventeen, and all she cared about were her friends. She abided by our rules, so I didn't have any complaints about her hanging out.

"Okay, I'm so excited!" I went into our bathroom to get ready for the day. I couldn't wait to drive around in my new whip. I wasted no time hitting the streets with plans to meet Casey back at home so we could go out, but my first stop was the nail shop. I needed a full set and a pedicure. While I was in the chair getting a pedicure, my phone vibrated. It was a weird number that I didn't have stored.

"Hello?"

"Happy Birthday, Baby." I damn near dropped my phone in the pedicure water at the sound of Eriq's voice. I was speechless. I had a lot to say to him, but didn't know where to start. I hadn't spoken to him in ten months.

"Eriq?" I had to confirm it was him, because I was in disbelief.

"Yea, it's me, where are you? Can we meet up?" he asked.

So many thoughts went through my head. I wanted to say yes, and a part of me wanted to hang up in his face. I didn't know if I should call Casey to tell him what was going on. I didn't want to get him fired up so I declined on that thought. I wanted to hear what he had to say. No matter how I felt, he was still Aden's biological dad.

"Meet me in front of your brother's house in an hour." I was nervous about seeing him, and I promised myself not to slap the shit out of him.

After getting my nails and toes did, I slid in my ELR and over to Sam's house. I didn't see Eriq's Monte Carlo, but I did see a Benz G Wagon parked in the driveway. I called the number that he called me from to let him know I was there. Before it had a chance to ring, I hung up because he was getting out of the Benz. My heart thumped in my chest as he walked up to my car. I swear I wanted to slap him, choke him, hell I wanted to shoot him. He looked into the car and smiled at me. His smile made me frown. It wasn't shit to be smiling about.

"What the fuck are you smiling about? Where have you been?"

I wasn't about to let him finesse his way back in like he had done in the past when we broke up. He paused and thought about his answer.

"I was gone building a better life for us. I wasn't no good to you or my son, so I had go out and get it for y'all. This was for y'all."

He lowered his head down into my car, and he was face to face with me.

"Regardless of what the streets said, or what you thought, I was grinding day in and out until I felt like it was enough to support what's mine."

I didn't want to hear shit he was saying. His explanation meant nothing to me.

"So you thought leaving me pregnant, in the fuckin projects, without knowing what happened to you was in the best interest for me and my son?" That shit made no sense to me.

"Baby, we have a house now, a big ass house, that truck and a few other cars, money in accounts, you name it, I got it for you. Shit, we can get married today. I was out there sacrificing whatever for you."

Tears began to stream down my face. Maybe if I was still in the projects where he had left me, this would have been music to my ears, because even with everything I had been through without him around, I still loved him. He was my first love, my child's father, my world at one point in my life, but things were different now. I had nice things, I had love, and I had a father for my son in the ten months that he was gone with no trace. God had blessed me with it all.

"This car is nice." he said and was now looking at me for answers.

"Thanks," was all I said to him.

"I went by your old crib and Ayesha told me y'all moved but wouldn't tell me where. And by Chicken Shack."

Thank God Ayesha didn't run her mouth to him.

"Yea, we moved out when Aden was born." I didn't want to be the bearer of bad news but he needed to know.

"Listen Eriq, when you left me, I didn't know if you was leaving me to be a single mother or what the case was."

I damn sure wasn't thinking I should hang out for months, have a baby alone, and raise him for eight months alone with the other kids while I wait for Eriq to return with the jackpot.

"I have someone in my life. We've been together a while now, and things are serious." I said looking him in the eye. He looked back at me like I had told him I killed his mama.

"So you telling me you throwing everything with us away for a new relationship?" he said sounding devastated, but I couldn't find it in me to care.

How he felt was nothing compared to what I had felt when he left me, and I wasn't about to let him down play my relationship with Casey.

"No, I'm telling you I moved on with a person that has been there for me when I was in my darkest hour. You wasn't there when I had to stab a nigga to keep him from killing my mama in my house. Or I don't remember you being there after the fact when I didn't have a place to live with three kids and a new born. You weren't there when I was in labor for nine hours, you weren't there for any of Aden's milestones. He was there, through it all, and he's still there for whatever it is I need."

Tears were streaming down my face, and I wanted to close this chapter and pull off, but I knew this was only the beginning. Eriq wasn't going to stop trying to get me back, and Casey damn sure wasn't handing me over.

"You have this nigga around my son? Who is he?"

I didn't want to put salt on a wound. He just didn't know Aden thought Casey was his daddy. We were way past the "a nigga around my son stage". I don't know if his ass realized he had been MIA for ten months, and his son was only eight months old. Aden had never laid eyes on Eriq.

"You have no one to blame for this but yourself. Aden is always around him. We all live together. We have been living together since he has been born." I wasn't going to lie to him. He needed to know the consequences of his actions.

"How the fuck have you lived with him since he's been born? You had to have been fuckin with the nigga when we were together to move on so fast."

I wasn't about to listen to this. I felt like this was the problem with most simple minded niggas. They could have a loyal, pure-hearted woman that's all for them, and when they fuck up causing the woman to move on, she instantly becomes a cheater, a hoe, or whatever. I didn't have a nigga on the side, nor did I pursue Casey. This all happened in divine order, and Eriq was now sick that the cards wasn't dealt they way he planned.

"I have to go Eriq. I'm willing to let you meet Aden. I will text you with a time that works best for my schedule." And with that, I drove off.

My blood was boiling; this nigga really had lost his mind. I didn't like the idea of keeping anything from Casey, so I decided to call him and tell him what was going on. I knew it probably would put a damper on my birthday plans, but honesty was always the best policy. Casey didn't answer when I called.

Well, off to the Salon to get my hair done. I thought.

I went to see Tricey for a full makeover. I hadn't been to see her since Aden was born, because I had been doing my own hair, and it was so long now that flat ironing it had become an all day job.

"Well, who is this stranger?" she joked as I walked over to her shampoo chair.

"It has been a minute. I was trying to lay low-key. You remember how it went down the last time I was here." All of the stylists laughed.

"Yea, Marquita had to beat a bitch down your last visit. You silly as hell girl." Tricey said, still laughing with tears.

As I sat in Tricey's chair listening to her complain about how long and untamed my hair was, I contemplated what style I wanted.

"Do what you feel with it; I know you got those magic hands."

"I'm about to chop it all off." she grabbed a handful of my hair and ran her fingers through it. case

"Go for it; just don't have me looking crazy." I trusted Tricey to slay me.

She was the best at what she did, and my hair grew like wildfire, so worse it would just grow back.

"So what you been up to girl?" She didn't waste no time digging in.

"The usual for me… work, school, taking care of my man and kids." I hated the gossip that came with going to get my hair did, but I loved the way I felt when I left up out of there.

"Yea, that's really all to do. Ain't shit poppin fareal. So I heard you and Case been serious. Good job, girl; he is a winner." she laughed.

I couldn't focus too much on what she was saying, because my hair was hitting the floor by the damn ounces, and I was starting to second guess the decision to cut my hair.

"Bridgette came here last week, and she was as big as a house. She told me they're little girl was due any day now."

I wasn't sure if Tricey had just told me that Casey and Bridgette were having a baby any day now. I couldn't have heard her right.

"What? She's pregnant by who? Case?" I asked confused as fuck. Tricey stopped talking. She was either being messy or she honestly didn't know that I was clueless to the fact.

"Um yea, that's who she said was her baby daddy. She's nine months now." Tricey said.

My vision went blurry, and my heart rate decreased. I wanted to run out that door full speed to find Casey and hurt him. Tricey was still talking to me, but I didn't hear a thing. I held my hand up to signal for her to shut the fuck up. The remainder of this appointment was going to be in silence.

I needed to talk to Casey first. Bridgette was a ratchet bitch that thrived off of attention, so Casey could have easily not been her child's father. When Tricey handed me the mirror, I wanted to kiss myself. She slayed my bob. It was cut to precision, and my wavy baby hairs were laid how I liked. My hair danced with the motion of my head.

"Damn, Bitch! You are a bad one." one of her other clients said.

"Thank you, I love it!"

My hair looked so good I forgot all about Bridgette and Casey's asses. I walked over to sit in Coco's chair for him to beat my face. I had never had a full face of makeup before, but I knew that Coco was great at what he did.

"I've been waiting to get my hands on this pretty lil face." he said batting his fake lashes.

"Not too much, Coco. You know I don't wear this shit." I laughed.

"Hush Chile and let me werk my magic."

Unlike Tricey's chair, Coco shared with me all his problems. He wanted everyone to be his psychologist. I thought being gay was about not having to deal with fuck shit from the opposite sex, but from the sound of his problems, that shit was beyond any stress level I could imagine. When he gave me the mirror, I wanted to cry. My brows were perfect, my skin tone was flawless, my lashes were dramatic, my lipstick accented my lips perfectly, and my contour was to die for.

"Boy! You got me fine as fuck." I couldn't believe that it was me in the mirror.

"You make me want to sample the cookie jar with your bad ass and that banging ass body." Coco joked.

I walked out of there feeling like I was that chick and I couldn't be touched. I didn't want to call Casey, but I did decide to show up to the barber shop where he was at. I needed to see his face when I confronted him with this shit. It was guy code that I didn't bring my ass to the barber shop, especially unannounced, but this was 911, and I didn't give a fuck about the guy code at this point. I walked into the shop, and every nigga in there had their eyes glued on me. They knew who I belonged, so they didn't dare say a word to me.

"Case is in his office." Butch, an old head that worked in Casey's shop, said to me.

All of the other barber's gave Butch a mugged look, because he told me where to find Casey. Feeling inferior, I walked right into his office, and low and behold he was in there with Bridgette. He looked angered talking to her, and she looked like a sad puppy. I closed the door behind me as I walked in. Casey's eyes widened and hers had a look of satisfaction.

"Don't let me disturb the two of you, continue on." I said, calmly, but really wanting to go into an outrage. I wanted answers, and if I went crazy on their asses, there was a chance that I wouldn't get what I came for.

"You look beautiful baby." Casey said, throwing me off guard. Bridgette gave him the look of death.

"Why is she here?" I had no time to play around with him. My birthday excitement was declining rapidly, because of the niggas in my life.

"She was just leaving." Casey said looking at her to agree with him.

"I asked you why the fuck is she here Casey?"

"She's pregnant as you can see Maliah, nine months...and she's claiming it is by me." It hurt me to the core hearing him say that, but I couldn't be as angry as I wanted to be with him. We weren't official nine months ago. He was with Bridgette's trashy ass.

She stood up to leave, and I wanted to slap the skin off her face for pulling this stunt, but looking at her and looking at me, I had already won.

She closed the door behind herself.

"Why didn't I know about this when you found out about it? I had to hear about the shit while I was getting my hair done."

I hated to be humiliated, and I really hated for someone to give information about my man that I didn't already know.

"I was going to tell you; I had to figure out what was going on first. There was no reason to turn my house upside down and her ass was lying."

His mouth was saying one thing, but his eyes were looking all over my body. I could tell that he was taken back by my new look. I was hearing every word he was saying and trying my best to be understanding.

"So do you think it's yours?" I really didn't want to know the answer to the question, but I needed to know. He rubbed his hands down his face and sat in his office chair.

"It's a possibility, but I don't know. I want you to know, though, I haven't fucked her since we been together. We will get a blood test once the baby is here."

He waved his hand signaling for me to come over to him. I followed his command, and he pulled me down into his lap.

"Don't worry about this; today is your day. If it's mine, I'm going to take care of it, but I'm done with her ass. That's not what you are going to worry about." I guess now was the time to tell him about Eriq.

"Eriq called me today, and he wanted to meet up with me." I wasn't sure how he would take the news, but I had to let him know.

"I know you ain't agree to meet up with the nigga." I took a deep breath before I answered.

"I met him at his brother's house after I left the nail shop." Casey screwed his face up at me like I was a disgusting sight to him.

"Why the fuck would you meet up with him? It's no reason for you to see him." He was pushing me off of his lap with ease.

"Casey, it was a reason; we do have Aden. I wanted to see what was his sorry excuse was for turning his back on his son." I explained to him not budging off of his lap.

"Nah, fuck that; ain't shit to talk about, and it damn sure ain't no reason to meet up, especially without me. Change your fuckin number. If he wants to see Aden, tell him to call me!"

I felt as though he was being ridiculous. This was bigger than Aden; he was worried about me running back to Eriq. I didn't want to argue with Casey on my birthday, and I damn sure didn't want to argue about Eriq or Bridgette's dusty ass.

"Okay, baby, I'll change it. It really was only about Aden. I didn't even get out my car." I said, kissing on his neck trying to help release all the tension and stress he had built up that quickly. The last thing he had to worry about was the next man.

"Yo, go lock that door." he demanded.

I stood up to do as I was told, then he slapped me on my ass. I wanted the dick, but I didn't want to sweat my hair out or smear my makeup, and that was bound to happen fucking with him. He sat back in his chair watching me like a hawk walk back over to him.

"I'm feeling this hair; it's sexy on you." he smiled.

"Baby, I don't want you to have me lookin like shit for the rest of the day." I whined. I knew I was about to walk out of that office looking fucked up if I let him have his way with me.

"I won't, I promise." he mumbled.

I straddled his lap and attacked him with a passionate kiss. As soon as our lips met, I felt my juices flow and my panties got moist. It felt like I was sitting on a brick, because he was standing at attention. He unbuckled my pants never pulling away from my kiss. He abruptly stood up and held me in the air, while still kissing me. He was a sex god, and I never knew what to expect when we were in the sheets. The shit drove me crazy. He laid me on my back on his desk finally breaking our kissing.

He tugged my pants halfway down and lifted my legs straight up in the air. He sat back down in his chair in front of me and began to feast in my pot of gold. It felt so good that a tear slipped out the corner of my eye. I didn't make a sound, because I knew if I did he would have no mercy down there.

Whenever we had sex in public, he would tell me not to make one sound. It was like winning the lottery and not being able to tell a soul. He stood up and pulled out his massive black dick, and with some force, he slid it in. My body complied with his with every hard stroke he was giving me.

He banged me so hard that I had to hold the edges of the desk to keep from sliding off the muthafucka. I bit my bottom lip as it trembled.

I was getting closer to releasing. He always wanted eye contact when I was cumming, and for some reason, it intensified the orgasm to heights that only one could dream of. I was climbing the wall with every stroke, as he picked up the pace and I finally got there. I nodded my head yes to him with tears welled up in my eyes. Silently, I had the most intense orgasm I had ever had in my entire nineteen years of life. I didn't know if it was because of the added tension we had just had before sex, but it was damn good like always, and every time was the best time.

On cue, when I was finished creaming, he busted a huge load inside of me. He made all kinds of noises, which I was sure informed everyone in the shop that we were fuckin. I slapped his arm.

"Why are you so damn loud? You know the rules; no sounds in public." I fussed.

"No, that rule applies to you." he said laughing.

He hated how I thought everything was embarrassing, so he intentionally did things to embarrass me or call me out. In his mind, that was his way of getting me out of caring about what other people thought. I walked into the bathroom connected to his office to take a hoe bath before leaving his office with the walk of shame which was not fun. Then, he walked me out to my car.

"I'll see you tonight." Casey said, kissing me before I got in the car. *Damn, I love that man.* I thought.

****

I was sipping my Apple Cîroc and feeling good. I had on my black Herve Leger dress and black Giuseppe Zanotti spiked heels. My hair was still in place, and I had powdered up my face for a fresher look. I was looking the best I had ever looked, but I didn't feel as good as I looked though.

I had so many emotions running through my mind. Seeing Eriq today had me feeling some type of way. I was happy with Casey, but the closure with Eriq wasn't exactly closure, and I didn't know if the feelings I once had for him would resurface. I pushed all of that to the side. It was my 19th birthday, and I was about to turn all the way up. The party bus made several stops to pick up Ayesha, Shawnie, and my girl, Tajha, who I went to school with. I was ready to party the night away.

"Ayesha, why you wear those damn flats?" She got on my nerves having us looking crazy as a unit every time we went out.

"Girl, I'm trying to be comfortable. Y'all can wear heels."

Who in the hell came to the club to be comfortable. Females wore open toes and miniskirts in the cold Michigan air to be cute, not comfortable. We stopped in front of the club, and the music was blaring on the outside. It was a long line wrapped around the club, but we all stepped out and walked past everyone to get to the front door. When I showed the bouncer my ID, he knew who I was and let me and my girls in. We got our VIP wrist bands and was escorted to the VIP section. The level was adorned with red and gold balloons and the bottle service was in full effect. A banner hung down facing the lower level that read Happy Birthday, Maliah.

"Damn girl, Case went all out for you." Shawnie said, dancing to Fetty Wap's song "Again".

My girls and I hit the dance floor and danced to every song the DJ put into rotation, and I hadn't had fun like this in a long time. As I was dancing, I felt an arm wrap around my waist, and I immediately stopped dancing to turn around to see who was daring enough to put their hands on me. I was slightly intoxicated so my reaction was slower than usual. I turned around to see Casey smiling at me, and he looked too good. He was always dapper, but right now, in this club, he had a bitch wanting to slide her panties off and assume the position.

He had on all white. The all white Hudson jeans, Versace gold and white t-shirt, white Maison Margiela shoes, and gold chains glowing under the club lights.

"You enjoying yourself?" His eyes were low from the premium marijuana and Hennessy he had been drinking.

"Yes, thank you for doing all of this for my birthday." I yelled over the loud music.

He took me by the hand and escorted me back to the VIP section he had set up for me.

"I have to go to the restroom I'll be right back."

I signaled for Ayesha to go with me. I was drunk but still alert and aware enough not to go to the bathroom alone. I would never let myself get too drunk that I couldn't look after myself. It took me longer than usual to use the restroom, mainly because I didn't want to assume I was that I was sober more than what I was and have an accident on myself.

"I'm so happy you're enjoying yo birthday." Ayesha said with her words a little slurred.

Everyone was taking advantage of the free alcohol, and she was no exception. As soon as I walked out of the bathroom, I ran into Eriq, and it was clear that he was wasted.

"What's up, baby? I heard this was yo party." he said, walking up to me and backing me into the wall.

I was now pinned between the wall and him. I could smell the alcohol all over him, and his slanted eyes were so low they looked closed.

"Eriq, you need to back up." I put my hand on his chest to push him back, but he didn't move.

"Nah, I'm not going nowhere; you need to come home with me…where you and my son belong."

I felt my body get aroused with him being so close to me; we hadn't been this close since I had last saw him, before he made his disappearance. He placed his hand on my thigh and that sent electricity straight to my pussy.

"Come home to daddy where you belong." he breathed in my ear. I stood there for a moment caught up in his fury.

I missed him, but he did me dirty, and now I wanted nothing more than to hate him.

"Maliah, you need to come on before Case comes over here and sees this shit," Ayesha said in my ear.

When I heard Casey's name, I snapped out of lust real quick. I knew if I was gone too long, he would come looking for me, and I didn't need those types of problems. I grabbed Eriq's hand off of my leg.

"I have to go." I left without giving him a chance to respond, but just like I expected, Eriq followed me.

"I wanna see who this nigga is that's keeping you from coming home with me." Eriq yelled following behind me.

I don't need this; it is my birthday, and this fool was getting ready to ruin it. I thought ready to cry.

How dare he impose on my life after I had gotten my shit together? He was the one that decided to leave me. I spotted Casey standing against the bar talking to one of the bartenders. He was probably ordering another round for everyone. Casey and I made eye contact, and he began to walk over to me. I could tell by his angered facial expression that he saw Eriq in tow.

I made it to where Casey was, and I immediately retrieved the shot of Patron he was holding in his hand. I no longer cared to be any ounce of sober. I didn't want no parts of this shit. I needed the alcohol to get me the hell up out of this situation.

"Yo, you fuckin around with this nigga?" Eriq yelled, still walking toward us laughing. I glanced over to Eriq and noticed Sam, Rodney, and Ed were making their way over to be by his side.

Oh, shit. His Brothers are here too. I thought. These Niggas all lived for drama.

Casey had fire in his eyes, and Eriq's eyes were pain-filled mixed with anger.

"Fuckin around? Nigga, she ain't fuckin around; that's my pussy," Casey fumed.

Those words sent Eriq in a frenzy. He charged at Casey like Bull. If he wasn't as drunk as he was, Casey would have been in trouble, because this nigga was straight in animal mode.

Casey got the fuck out of dodge, pulled his gun out, and jammed it to the side of Eriq's temple. Sam, Ed, and Rodney stood there with guns drawn at Casey, but each of them had red dots on their chest. My eyes roamed the club to see if I could spot who had them targeted. All I could do was pray that no one got hurt. I couldn't believe I was the cause of all of this commotion. I don't know if it was the alcohol or what, because Eriq remained calm and didn't flinch or tense up.

"Listen up, nigga. She ain't yours; she's mine. Always will be. I'm willing to die over what's mine and you ain't, so you better think about what you just got yourself into bo-"

Before Eriq could get his word out, Casey hit him in the head with the butt of his gun. Eriq's head began to ooze blood, as the crowd rushed in. The liquor was starting to take a heavy effect on me, but I rushed to Eriq's side to make sure he didn't fall and hit his head on the club's concrete floor. It had to have been a natural reaction for me to help him, because my better judgment would have been to leave with Casey and not look back.

Once my mind focused in on what I was doing, it was too late. I made eye contact with Casey, who was signaling for me to come on, because someone has mentioned the police. He saw that I was kneeling down attempting to console Eriq, and he gave me a cold look before turning his back. He disappeared in the crowd, and I was hot on his tracks to explain. I couldn't find anyone. Ayesha, Shawnie, or Tajha were nowhere in sight.

"Where the fuck are they?" I asked myself. I retrieved my phone from my purse to call Ayesha after seeing I already had twelve missed calls from her.

"Maliah!" she said in a panic.

"Where are y'all at?" I asked.

"We all made it to the party bus one by one, and Case said that you were riding with him, but when I saw him hop in the car without you, I got worried. Are you okay?" she asked and stated all in one breathe.

I was in a state of shock that he had left me in all of this chaos alone. I could here gunshots ringing in the club, and by then, the police had the place surrounded.

"I'm about to request me an Uber; I'll be fine. I'll call you when I make it home." I hung up with her and started walking in the opposite direction of the club.

I couldn't believe Casey had left me there, and I couldn't believe I had ran to Eriq's side before his. I was upset about how the entire situation had played out. The Uber arrived within five minutes of my request, and when I got home, it was to an empty house. I had called Casey a thousand times on my ride home. It rang the first ten times I called, but the rest all went straight to voicemail.

I knew he was mad at me, but my safety should have still been important to him. I was not expecting my birthday to end like this. I walked in our bedroom, and there were over ten dozen roses over the room in vases. Our bed was stacked with Chanel Perfume and designer handbags. Casey had this laid out for me to come home to after we left the club. I immediately broke down into tears.

I kicked myself for trying to help Eriq when he was the dumbass that put himself in this shit. I had a good man that did nothing but try to make me, my son, and my siblings happy. I sprawled out across my bed next to the pile of gifts and cried my eyes out until I fell asleep.

The next morning, I woke up to still an empty house. I had no missed calls from Casey, so I decided to shower and go pick up the kids before I had a meltdown. A part of me wanted to know if Eriq was okay. I knew better than to call around asking and risk word getting back to Casey. I drove up to Casey's mothers house and noticed his car in the driveway. The pain in my heart slowly eased seeing he had been here all along with his mom and the kids.

I knocked on the door for what seemed to be too damn long for a house full of people to have been there. Just as I was getting ready to knock again, his mama answered the door.

"Hi, Mrs. Rice." She was still standing in the door hesitant to let me in. "I came to pick up the kids." I announced.

She widened the door to let me in. It was toys sprawled out all across her living room indicating the kids had a good time. Kayla came walking out of the kitchen eating a can of Pringles.

"Hey, Maliah." she said with a mouth full of chips.

"Hi. Girl, take those chips back to the kitchen, you're dropping crumbs everywhere." I scolded her.

"Where is everyone?" I asked Mrs. Rice, who was not being her talkative self.

"Casey and Aden are upstairs sleeping, and Jaylen is in the backyard with the basketball." she said. "I can tell you've been crying, Maliah. Come sit in here and talk to me," she said walking toward her office. She closed the door behind her, and I broke down crying the moment I sat down. I was crying mostly because I was scared and confused. I was the cause of all of this drama, and I hated it.

I obviously still had love for Eriq, and that was why I showed concern for him at the club. I felt like shit afterwards, because I had hurt the one person that showed the most love and care for me.

"Listen, Maliah, I know you have a lot on your plate, and you are a strong young lady." I wiped my eyes with the back of my hands to listen to what she was saying. "I told Casey from the day he showed signs of interest in you that you had too much on you and to leave you alone. He has a lot going for himself Maliah. He has businesses, investments, no kids, and I raised him up to be a fine young man. He doesn't need to be in clubs fighting and stressing over you."

I was shocked at what she was saying. The blow she was throwing was painful, but she was right. I didn't need Casey in this mess. I was confused and had issues I needed to sort out.

"You need to figure things out with your child's father and leave Casey out of it. If you need some financial help, help with kids, or a place to stay, I can help you. I have a few properties you can stay in until you get yourself together."

I didn't need her hand outs. I only felt what she was saying, because I loved Casey and wanted the same for him, but she wasn't going to treat me like a charity case after telling me I wasn't good enough for her son. I stood up and pulled myself together I didn't want the kids to see me broken.

"Kayla, go get Jaylen and put your shoes on." I called out to her.

As I entered the bedroom where Aden and Casey were sleeping, I felt tears threatening to fall again. Aden's little body was curled under Casey, and the both of them snored away. Casey still had on his clothes from the club. I bagged up Aden's things that were laying around the room, and I tried being as quiet as possible, but that didn't stop Casey from waking up.

"What are you doing?" he asked groggily.

"About to take the kids home." I said still collecting his items.

"I was bringing them home; you ain't have to come here." he said in the nastiest tone.

"Well, since you weren't answering your phone, I didn't have any way of knowing that." I carefully picked up Aden making sure I didn't wake him. Casey stared at his vibrating phone that he was holding. After examining the number, he answered.

"Hello?"

"Word? Where she at?"

"Alright, I'll be there." He ended the call just as quick as he answered it.

"I'm out of here." he announced. When he walked over to me, he bent down to kiss Aden's head and left the room.

"Where are you going?" I asked. He didn't bother answering me. I watched him tell his mother and the kid's bye before he left. Jaylen and Kayla were all ready to go.

"Thanks for keeping them." I mumbled to Mrs. Rice. The kids hugged her and we left.

During the ride home I couldn't help but wonder where Casey was heading to. He didn't take a shower or change his clothes. I tried calling him, but he had turned his phone back off. I decided to take my mind off of everything by going home to make a homemade pizza with the kids. To my surprise, Marquita was home when I got there. I was expecting her to be gone all weekend.

"Are you okay?" she asked me as soon as I walked in the door.

"I'm fine, why?" I asked confused.

"I heard about all the drama at the club." I'm sure by now it wasn't too many people out there that hadn't heard about what went on.

"Yea, I'm cool." I reassured her.

"Where is Case?" she asked.

"I have no idea where he is." I explained to her what all that happened at the club not sparing any details.

Later that night, after the kids were sleep, I tried to call Casey and still got no answer. I decided to do something I hadn't done in a long time, and that was log into Facebook. I scrolled through all the fakes and the social media lies they told until I landed on Mrs. Rice's page, and there were pictures of her holding a baby girl with the caption, "My first Grandbaby". I damn near dropped my phone.

The baby she was holding looked just like Casey, and I could see him slightly in the background.

"What the fuck?" I said to myself. I was so angry my hands were trembling. I searched Bridgette's name on Facebook, and although we weren't friends, she was messy enough to make all the baby's pictures public. She had pictures of Casey holding her baby with the caption

"Twins" and "My little family". I called him repeatedly and only got his voicemail. Then, I called Mrs. Rice and she sent me to voicemail.

As bad as I wanted to cry, I didn't. I was tired of crying. I took Aden out of his bed and cuddled with him until I finally went to sleep.

Casey didn't come home for four days, nor did he call me. I felt the same feeling overcome me from when Eriq left me. I couldn't take being in the house any longer so after work, I decided to stay at Ayesha's house and chilled with her. Her mama watched the kids for me while I worked.

"I can't believe he is over there playing house with that bitch." I said to Ayesha as she smoked a blunt. I wasn't a smoker, but I was drowning in the Patron bottle.

"Fuck him and her; you can stay here until you get your house." Ayesha said, blowing smoke from her mouth. I nodded my headed contemplating her offer.

We sat on her porch for hours talking about the same topic as the sound of Future's "Lie to Me" blared from the G-wagon that parked in front of Ayesha's townhouse.

"Oh, shit, that's Eriq." I said to her. I stood up to go in the house hoping he didn't see me, but I had consumed too much liquor, and my body was not moving as fast as I would have liked to. He hopped out of the truck with it still running.

"Maliah, let me holla at you." he said approaching the house.

Just months ago, I couldn't find the nigga to save my life, but now he seemed to be everywhere I was at. I took off in the house.

"I'm not leaving this bitch until I talk to you." he yelled.

"Girl, just talk to the nigga, and get his ass off my porch." Ayesha said, walking in her house.

"I don't have shit to say to him." I said waving her off.

"Maliah, I will walk in this muthafucka." he yelled in the screen door.

I know he was trying to be respectful, because he had no problem coming in her house if it meant shooting the hinges off the door. All I could think about was the kids in the back playing. I didn't need this mess around them. I opened the door and closed it behind me. He had a knot on his forehead and stitches, I assumed from being hit with the gun by Casey.

"Damn, I gotta do all this to holla at you?" I rolled my eyes at his comment.

"What the hell do you want?" I asked stepping out of the house onto the porch with him. I was regretting staying over here. I should have took my ass home.

"Maliah, I need to meet my son. If you want that bitch nigga, fine, but you crazy as fuck if you think I'm not about to be a part of my baby's life.

"Eriq, you chose not to be a part of Aden's life, not me." I huffed.

"I'm done explaining what the fuck I had to do. I'm not asking you, I'm telling you to let me see him, and why the fuck did you name him Aden?"

I wanted to knot the other side of his fucking head. If he wanted to meet Aden, I was going to let him. Aden wasn't for no games. If he didn't know you, he wasn't messing with you, and Eriq was about to find out real quick. I went in the house to get him. When I got to the back room, Kayla was holding him and watching The Disney Channel. He cooed at the sight of me.

"Come on, Mama's man." I picked him up, and Ayesha looked at me like I was crazy when I walked past her toward the front door.

I walked back outside with Aden on my hip. He looked at Eriq, and instantly, hugged onto me tighter. Eriq stood up and stared at him. He didn't say anything for minutes.

"Hey." he said attempting to hold his hand, but Aden snatched it away.

"Let me hold him." Eriq said, holding his arms out to take him.

"He's not going to come to you." He gently grabbed him out of my arms, and Aden went crazy. He stiffened his body and started yelling at the top of his lungs. I chuckled to myself.

"Give him here." I said.

"Nah, he cool." he insisted.

"Aye man, what's with all this crying? Why you doing all this? Ya mama got you up under her all day being a sucka?" Aden heard his voice and looked up at his face.

"Yea, you know this daddy talking." Eriq laughed. Eriq sat there and talked to Aden, and he hung onto every word he was saying without fussing.

"When are you coming home with me, Maliah?" he asked, breaking his attention from the baby. "You said you wanted to see Aden, so enjoy him."

"So what? You think you're about to play family with my son, and that's it? That nigga is about to catch a hot one, so my advice to you is don't get too attached." I looked at him in disbelief.

"Rather than be acting a damn fool, you should be thanking him. Something could have happened to us while you were gone." He looked at me and then back down at Aden, who had fallen asleep in his arms.

"I didn't fully think this through. I didn't consider the fucked up shit that could have occurred when I left. I was only thinking about the future. I was not for being a broke bum ass father. That wasn't an option for me. It's fucked up, you can't understand that."

"It's not the fact that you wanted better. The issue here is that you didn't tell me shit. You hung me out there to dry and Case-."

"Fuck that nigga. He knew we were together. He's a bitch ass nigga that waited for me to dip outta town to slide through and scoop your silly ass, and you fell for it. He knew exactly where the fuck I was at; his mama was my connect. At any time, he could have told me what popped off at yo mama spot, and I would have easily came home and handled it, but the nigga had his own plan." he vented.

I felt like a fool. Casey knew where Eriq was all this time? His mama is a king pin? So many thoughts raced through my head. I was betrayed in the worst way if any of what Eriq was telling me was true.

"Eriq, it's getting late, and I have to go put them to bed; they have school." I was ready to have a breakdown, and I needed to get out of his presence.

"When am I going to see my baby again?" he asked not wanting to give Aden over.

"Call me tomorrow after four, and I'll meet you somewhere," I said, taking my baby out of his arms.

"I ain't got your number; you changed it." he said persistently. I ratted out my number to him and went in the house to get my sister and brother.

I drove home in silence letting every situation play in my head. Was this situation with Eriq and Casey deeper than me and I was just a pawn in the game? I thought about Mrs. Rice's words to me earlier that week.

I was upset with myself for placing my family in a bullshit situation. Was I really that shallow minded?

As soon as I got to the condo, I had the kids grab some clothes and toys, and I would pick Marquita up from her friend's house on my way to the hotel where we would be staying at. I was so happy that I didn't junk my Focus like I started to do. I didn't know if Casey had a tracking device on the vehicles that he had purchased for me. I packed Aden and myself some clothes in a duffle bag.

I was leaving all of these niggas behind me. I apparently was too kindhearted and getting fucked over every which way I turned. I opened the bedroom door to gather the kids and leave. I would get the rest of our things at a later date. When I went to open the door, Casey stepped in.

"Where are you going this late?" he questioned, looking at the duffle bags hanging off my shoulder. I attempted to walk past him when he grabbed my arm with force.

"I asked you a question." he said with venom in his voice. I had never been scared of him nor questioned his intentions until now.

"I'm leaving Casey." I said not backing down to him.

"We can talk about this. Go in the room; the kids don't need to hear us talk. They need to be sleep; they have school in the morning." he said, nodding his head to the bedroom door.

"Casey!" Kayla squealed rubbing her sleepy eyes.

"Hey, baby girl. What are you doing up so late?" he asked picking her up.

"We are about to leave." she responded, resting her head on his shoulder. He cut his eyes at me.

"No, it's too late for you to go anywhere. The only place you're going is to bed" He carried her to her room and laid her in the bed.

I dropped my bags on the hallway floor, then he nodded in the direction of the room again, and I went inside to wait for him. I had class in the morning, so I didn't have time to talk to him all night about anything. I dug through the dresser drawer for a nightgown.

"Where exactly was you leaving to this time of night?" he asked, sitting on the edge of the bed.

"To a hotel, until I got my own place." I said not wanting to look at him.

"You seem to think this is a fuckin game or some shit." I wasn't sure what he was referring to because none of this was a game to me.

"What are you talking about Casey?"

"You was with that nigga tonight." he stated, looking at me with a dumbfounded expression. *How the fuck did he know that?* I thought.

"How would know since you was too busy playing daddy with ya bitch?" I said frustrated.

He stood up and walked close up on me. He put his forehead up to mine and through gritted teeth, he said "I don't give a fuck what you assume I was doing. I told you not to let that nigga around Aden unless I was there. And you did what the fuck you wanted. You know what; you can get the fuck out. You're not dragging the kids with you, but you can go. I should have left yo ass in the streets where that nigga left you." His last choice of words sent me over the edge.

I jumped up over him and swung aiming to hit him in the face. He caught my hand and pinned me down on the bed.

"You better calm the fuck down before you wake my son up."

"He's not your fuckin son, and I'm not your bitch! You just left from what's yours. You're over there playing house with the next, and you have the audacity to be in my face trying to run shit. On top of all your fuck shit, I was a part of your game? Your punk ass held me while I cried a river and you knew exactly where my baby daddy was? Fuck you, Casey, fuck you!" He released my arm and sat up in the bed.

"I wasn't playing house. I was making sure that my daughter was straight. She's mine, Maliah. The test came back and I'm her daddy."

My heart couldn't take much more; I didn't want to hear anything else that he was going to say.

"And I wasn't laid up with Bridgette. I seen the baby during the day and went to crash at my mom's house at night. I needed a few days to clear my head. You ran to that nigga's side over mine." he said with hurt in his voice.

"That's the thing, I wasn't choosing sides Casey. What you failed to realize is, regardless of the circumstances, Eriq is Aden's biological dad, and you two were in the club behaving like animals. No matter what hurt he caused me, or the fact that I have moved on, I didn't want to see him with his head split open. Hell, I would have helped anyone in that situation knowing me and my heart. You took it out of context, and for Aden's sake, we all need to get our shit together." I was becoming tired of the entire situation.

"I can't handle him being around y'all." he admitted.

"I knew where the nigga was at, but so what. What he did was some bitch made shit. It's no way in hell I'm leaving you for a minute in the hood alone with me being fully aware of what happens in the hood. Shit, I hate when you over Ayesha's crib. Muthafucka's get raped, killed, beat every day over there. I can never respect a man that would leave his woman in a fucked up predicament like that. You needed me, and I was going to be there for you, no matter what anyone had to say about it." I let his words soak in.

He had a valid point. It wasn't for him to tell me where to find my man. What Eriq did was unjustifiable, and I had to stop letting him get in my head.

"These few days have been long and I'm tired." I managed to say. I hadn't slept well in days.

Our life was good just last week, and now everything was a mess. I grabbed my nightgown off the bed and headed for the shower. I had to let the stress run off of me under some streaming hot water. I pulled Casey by the hand to shower with me, and he obliged and stood up to follow. That night, I still didn't sleep well I had too many negative thoughts consuming my mind.

Although Casey and I were back on good terms, there were so many things that didn't set well with me. I wanted to know how Casey knew that Eriq had seen Aden. I mean, we were smack dead in the hood where everyone was, but I didn't like the idea of someone running to him with my every move.

Chapter 16: Case

I had been spending more time with Bridgette and less time at home lately. It had nothing to do with me not wanting Maliah anymore; I couldn't take the idea of her creeping around Eriq's bitch ass. She thought that I was stupid and didn't know half the shit that went on. I had invested too much of my energy, time, and money to be made a fool out of.

I figured by me distancing myself from her that she would see I wasn't for the games. It was only a matter of time before I was back messing back around with Bridgette. All of the late night phone calls, and her swearing it was regarding my baby sucked me in. She knew Maliah and I were having issues, but she continued to use it to her own personal advantage.

I couldn't place all of the blame on her. I knew exactly what type of shit she was on, but I still chose to go with it.

I sat on the couch at Bridgette's crib rocking Cailey to sleep. When I was around her, I couldn't put her down or stop staring. I was infatuated with my baby girl. The feeling that she gave me was the same feeling that I got from Aden. There was nothing that I wouldn't do for my kids.

"How late are you staying?" Bridgette asked me, breaking the trance that Cailey had me under.

"I'm about to slide right now"

I stood up to take Cailey to her bedroom. I had spent the entire day there, and it was time for me to go home. Maliah didn't nag me all day asking me where   I was at, or who I was with, but I knew it bothered her. I needed to make peace at home, and the first step was to go there at a decent time.

Bridgette came into the bedroom with her arms folded and attitude on 100.

"Man, if you don't take yo ass out of here with all of that." The last thing that I was about to do was argue with her over my baby.

I walked out of the room and grabbed my keys off of the coffee table.

"When are you going to stop playing with me Case? I don't know how much of this I can take. Do you know how it makes me feel when you leave out of here to go be with her when I've been here for years? How the fuck did I get turned into the side bitch?" she cried.

I didn't feel bad, because she put herself in this. I didn't want to be in a relationship with her, and Cailey was not going to change that. Even after making this shit clear to her, she still continued to plot and scheme, but it wasn't happening. The relationship days for us was over.

"The fastest way for you to let it go is to accept it for what I've been telling you. You keep trying to keep me chained down here with pussy and my daughter, and I'm gone always be here for mine, but I ain't fuckin around with you like that Bridgette.

"That's what you keep saying, but you still fuckin me. You still paying my bills, you still ignoring ya bitch's phone calls when you are with me." She was clapping her hands and getting loud. I hated a pathetic woman; it had to be the biggest turn-off for me.

"Bridgette, get some sleep. I'll holla at you tomorrow."

She was still running off at the mouth, only I couldn't hear her crazy ass anymore. I had to get home to make things right.

When I got home, I could hear music blasting when I pulled into the garage. I don't know if it was the fact that my condo was live as hell at this time of night or the song of choice and its lyrics that was pissing me off. Bryson Tiller's "Let 'em Know" hit me as soon as I opened the door.

I'm coming back for good
So let them niggas know it's mines
Already got someone that's what you tell 'em every time
That shit ain't up for grabs

When I opened the door, I was met by Maliah and Marquita. Maliah was dressed in some sexy shit like she was about to get out the house for the night.

Neither one of them looked happy to see me which made me even angrier.

"What's going on up in here?" I questioned.

"I'm getting ready to go out; I'm surprised you decided to come home."

I never told her where she could and could not go, but tonight, her ass was not leaving the house.

"Go where, with who?"

"I'm going out with Ayesha." she said rolling her eyes.

Let me talk to you in the room please." I tried my best to remain calm. She hadn't done anything wrong, but my insecurities were running deep.

"I don't like you hanging with her. I've been telling you this shit for too long now."

"You can't come into my life, Casey, and tell me who I can and can't talk to." she said annoyed.

"I ain't telling you who you can talk to; I'm telling you that she can't be trusted."

She began to laugh like I had said the funniest joke that she had ever heard.

"She can't be trusted? Says the nigga that is cheating on me with his fuckin baby mama. You got your nerve coming in here tryin to get me to stay home after being out there living dirty all day."

I already knew that it was no rationalizing with her. Once she had her case going against me, there was no defending myself, because she wasn't backing down for shit.

The best thing that I could do was take what she was saying and let her do her thang. I trusted her; it was niggas that I didn't trust, or Ayesha's snake ass.

I took a shower and chilled in the bed with Aden until I fell asleep while she left to do what it was that she had her mind set on.

The next morning, I woke up to Maliah in bed with me. She was fully clothed in her attire from last night with her face planted in the pillow, and she had clearly had too much to drink. Marquita was in the living room with the kids.

I checked my phone and had a 911 text from PJ to meet him in the hood. He never texted me with urgency unless it meant serious business. My plan was to stay home all day and show Maliah that I was trying to make an effort to make things right, but here I was out the door before she was awake.

~~~~~~

"Nigga, a narc was just through here looking for you, and Nard. Asking us questions and shit about how often y'all come through here." Project said.

Nard was my stepbrother, and he was heavy in the streets. He was never on the scene of this hood ever, so I didn't understand why his name was being mentioned. I was nervous about a narc looking for me, because they were so far off if they thought that I dealt drugs. I was as clean as it came, but the shit didn't stop me from being noid for my family.

"And Rose is still out here trying us. Reggie caught her with an eight-ball in her shirt that she tried to get away with the other day. It's only gone be a matter of time. In her mind, she got away with it the first time, so you know she gone keep trying, nigga."

The news he was dropping on me was heavy. I was trying to make shit with Maliah right, so I had talked myself out getting Rosie touched, but this was the last straw.

"Alright, bro. Good lookin. I need to get the fuck from around here and lay low until we get this shit in order."

I parted ways with him and began to put my plan into motion.

Chapter 17: Maliah

The last few months had been difficult for us. I compromised with Casey on me taking Aden to see Eriq, but his terms were only in public places for a few hours. That was exceptionally easy since I didn't trust being alone with Eriq.

It wasn't that I thought he would do something to hurt Aden or me; I just didn't trust myself. He still had a tiny fraction of my heart, and being around him during the visits brought down the wall I built to block him out.

Casey had been spending more time with Baby Cailey and Bridgette, and I still had not seen the baby, and she was now five months old. We would stay arguing about him always having to run over Bridgette's house to see Cailey. She was old enough for him to bring her over to our house. He had set up all of these limitations for Eriq and me, but he was parading around town with his baby mama without a care in the world. It was safe to say that we were growing apart.

I was at Shawnie's apartment doing crafts for Aden's 1st birthday party next month. We had started hanging out more since Marquita had moved out and was attending college at Wayne State University down in Detroit, so I was alone most of the time with kids and needed the company.

"I can't believe he's about to be one." Shawnie said, opening a sucker for Aden since he was crying and falling out on the floor for it.

"Yes, this year flew by, and he's so damn spoiled. I can't do shit with him." I said, shaking my head at his behavior. Once Shawnie popped the sucker in his mouth, he sat up and started smiling.

"So are you inviting Eriq to his party?"

"Hell no; I'm not having him and Casey there together so they can ruin my baby's party." I scrunched my face at the idea. "We are going to have cake and ice cream with Eriq on his actual birthday solo." Eriq had been trying to step up and be there with the limited time he was given. If I needed something for my baby, he made sure to get it to me.

"That's cool; y'all are all working together with co-parenting. Mrs. Rice had a dinner at her house for her husband last night, and Bridgette was there with the baby. Casey wasn't there, though, so I figured he was at home with you." Shawnie stayed giving me the tea.

We had gotten into a big fight this morning, because he didn't come home until eight in the morning. He had given me some bullshit excuse about how he was chillin with his boy Kenny and a few other niggas and was too drunk to drive home, but I didn't share this with Shawnie.

My life was a mess already, so I didn't need people in my business. My intuition was telling me that Casey was fucking Bridgette, but I tried my best not to entertain my assumptions.

"His mama is crazy about the baby; she looks just like their asses." she said.

"Tell me about it; she posts one hundred pics a day of her." I agreed with her.

Since my last encounter with Mrs. Rice, I didn't have much to say to her. She made herself clear how she felt about me, and I wasn't in the business of kissing ass. The kids loved her, and they cried every weekend to go over to her house, so I would have Casey drop them off so I didn't have to see her. I had my own mama to worry about, because she was back in the rehabilitation center.

This time, she checked herself in. She told me she was tired of running from her problems and wanted to get clean. I went to visit her and keep her company every day. I wanted her to know that I was there to support her in her decision.

When I got home late that evening, Casey was home with the kids. He picked them up from school and took Jaylen to basketball practice. Even with all of the problems that we were having, his commitment was still in place with the kids. Aden was now walking, and the second his little feet hit the floor, he was walking over to Casey.

"What's up, Man?" he asked Aden, picking him up in his arms. He leaned over to me and gave me a dry peck on the lips. I wanted to tell him he could have kept that bullshit ass kiss, but I was tired and not in the mood to be pissed off.

"Where y'all was at?" he asked, giving Aden a boneless chicken wing out of the Buffalo Wild Wings carton that he was eating out of.

"At Shawnie's prepping for the birthday party." He gave me a blank stare and walked out of the kitchen. As he walked out, Jaylen walked in. He was now thirteen and was taller than me. His voice had changed, and acne had invaded his face.

"How was practice today?" I asked, as I watched him rumble through the bag of food for more chicken.

"It was cool; coach had me running more plays with the team." He was the starting point guard and was damn good at it. Casey had him in basketball camp all summer and that took his skills to another level.

"That's good; I can't wait to see you play Saturday." I smiled.

I roamed the condo looking for Kayla, and I should have known she was in her bed sleeping. She slept more than anyone in the house. Her hair was wild and curly, and her face was buried down in a Hello Kitty pillow. I couldn't help but laugh. Second grade wore her out every day. Back in our room, Aden was jumping in our bed like a mad man, and Casey was locked in on ESPN.

"Aden!" I yelled. He stopped jumping and looked at me like he was busted. "Stop jumping in the bed. Casey, you have no control over him." I said, shaking my head.

"He cool; he was having fun. Aye, I need to holla at you." He had my full, undivided attention. I never knew what to expect from him these days.

"I found us a new spot, over in Fenton. We are moving in two weeks." I didn't know how to react to the news. He was barely home now, so the last thing I was expecting was for him to tell me that we were moving.

"Why are we moving, and you can't seem to remember where you live at now?" I retorted.

"Who says I will remember after we move? My kids need more space. Their own backyard to play in. That's what this move is about."

It was unreal how distant he had become compared to how attached he was in the beginning. We went wrong the second Eriq came back into the picture. Casey hated that I was allowing him in Aden's life. Eriq fucked up the first eight months, but I couldn't deny him the rest of Aden's life. Rather than respond to his remark, I prepared for bed.

That night, I purposely wore something sexy to sleep. We hadn't had sex in over a week, which was the main reason behind my cheating accusations. Casey was the type of man that craved sex. He could never have enough of it, and for him not to have touched me this long, I knew something was off. When I came out of the bathroom, he was sitting on the chaise in our bedroom tying his shoes.

"Casey, I know you are not getting ready to leave the house this late."

I felt my blood pressure slowly rising. I had on some lace boy shorts and a matching lace push-up bra ready to fuck, and he was ready to walk out the door.

"I'll be right back. I gotta shoot a move real quick ." he said, barely paying me any attention.

"It's one in the morning. What moves are you making?" I grimaced.

"Man, watch out. I just told you I'll be right back. I won't be gone long." He brushed past me as he went through the house and out the side door. Casey had a problem with being questioned, and that was something I was not willing to compromise with him on. People that didn't want to be questioned didn't need to be in a relationships, was my theory.

My heart was heavy as I turned off the light and curled up in my bed. If someone would have told me my life would be like this in a year, I would have laughed in their face.

I was in a deep sleep that night when I felt Casey's head between my legs attacking my clit with his mouth. Initially, I thought I was dreaming, but after I adjusted my eyes and focused on the feeling, I realized it was real. He pushed my legs back and proceeded to lick and suck away. I didn't want to wake the kids, so I muffled my cries with a pillow.

I felt all of the stress and frustration I had built up over the past few weeks release my body as I reached my peak. I locked my legs around his head and covered his face with my juices. He came up for air and positioned me on my side so that he could slide into me from the back. I closed my eyes as we both enjoyed the feeling of each other's body. The sex was always passionate coming from him. Tonight, it was almost as if he was asking me for forgiveness using his body.

I woke up to one of those mornings where Aden wanted to run around the house playing, and Jaylen took forever in the shower. Casey had given me the address and key to check out the new house, but it bothered me that he never consulted with me on major decisions. Everything was his way or nothing.

After dropping Kayla and Jaylen off, I debated on taking Aden to daycare or letting him stay with me for the day. I quickly dismissed the thought of him staying with me after he launched his sippy cup across the truck. *I won't get anything done with him terrorizing.* I thought.

The new house was not too far from his daycare, and that was definitely an added bonus. As I entered the gated community, I took in how beautiful the houses were. It was definitely an upgrade from our condo. I was driving by houses that had to been valued at over a half million dollars, until Siri informed me that I had arrived at my destination.

I parked my SUV and sat there admiring the house. Everything about it was beautiful, from the landscaping, to the detailed architecture. I finally got out to enter my new domain, and when I entered the house, I damn there fainted. Coming from a dirty ass neighborhood and sharing a room with my sisters and brother, this was heaven.

The floors were marbled with cream and rich bronze, and upon entering, I was greeted by an imperial staircase. I continued to tour the house, and by the end, I had fell in love with the five bedrooms, four bathrooms, a private lake in the backyard, crystal chandeliers, and a walk-in closet fit for a Queen. When Casey said we had a new home, this was far beyond what I had imagined.

I loved him, and I was beyond grateful for him, but as I was sitting on the stairs in this beautiful house crying tears of joy, it made me realize I really didn't know him like I thought I did. He was twenty-six years old now, and obviously had more money than I could factor. I was aware that he owned a barbershop and he hustled here and there, but it wasn't adding up. He was such a humble person that hearing him boast and brag about materialistic things and how he made his money wasn't likely.

I thought back to Eriq telling me that Mrs. Rice was his connect. I never mentioned it to Casey, because we had enough drama going on that I didn't want to keep pressing what was already an issue. All of these thoughts invaded my mind, and I needed answers. I wasn't going to be the dizzy woman that didn't know shit about her man other than what he put in front of me. When I went to call him, he didn't answer. I left him home sleeping, so I figured that that was where he was. I quickly found out differently when I got home, and he was long gone.

"What the fuck?" I asked myself. I was so tired of playing this cat and mouse game with him. Today I was going to change up my daily routine. I called the attorney I worked for and told him that I would be working out of the office today at home. I knew exactly where Bridgette lived, but I told myself that I had no reason to ever go to where she resided.

I was done playing the fence if he didn't want to answer my calls or want to talk crazy to me and leave and at all hours of the night. I was going to demand the same respect that he was asking of me. If the shoe was on the other foot, he would be hounding my ass down before I even made it to where I was going. I got in my car and drove across the city to where she lived.

Shawnie had told me a while ago where the house was when I was contemplating being messy in the past, but I decided against it. There was no changing my mind today. When I made it to her house, Casey's car was in her driveway. Anger and all types of ill thoughts began to fill by body. I parked down the street to avoid him seeing me. I didn't want to go banging on the door, and worst case, they didn't answer, and I was left outside looking stupid, so I patiently waited for him to come out.

After sitting in the car, I began to think I could be sitting out there for hours. Forty minutes had already went by when I decided to go to the door and demand answers. I didn't care if I looked crazy or stupid. I was hurt and angry. I went to get out of the car when her front door opened, so I hurried and got back in my car before he saw me.

She walked out looking basic as hell, and he trailed behind her carrying the car seat with the baby in it. I punished myself by sitting there and watching them be the perfect family. They laughed as he put the baby in the back of her car. I watched him hug her and opened the door for her to get in the driver's seat. After he closed the door behind her, she lowered the window and said something to him that had him laughing harder than I had seen him laugh in a while.

I picked up my phone to call him, and I watched him retrieve his phone from his pocket, look at it, then place it back in his pocket. My heart was tired; it had been tossed in the air and shot at for too long now. I wanted to run over to him and slap the smile off of his face.

She pulled off, and he got in his car to leave. I sat there for what felt like hours before I left. I drove with no destination, until I decided to go see Ayesha. I hadn't seen her in a while, and I needed someone to talk to.

"Hey stranger, Where have been?" she asked as I walked in.

"Around; you know, doing the usual." I shrugged.

I hadn't talked to her in a few weeks since we last went out to the club. I had been going through so many problems myself that I had isolated myself from the world.

"What's wrong? I can tell something is fuckin with you." she observed. I plopped down on her couch preparing to tell her all my business when my phone alerted me that I had a text. It was Eriq asking if he could see Aden after I picked him up from daycare. I replied to him that I wasn't feeling good, and that we could meet up tomorrow.

"So what's wrong girl?" she asked waiting on my reply.

"So much has been going on. We are getting ready to move soon, and I don't know where my relationship stands." I said crying.

"Move? Where are you moving to? And what do you mean?" she asked hugging me. I didn't know why Casey's voice entered my head about telling no one where we live, but it did.

"Not too far." I murmured. We were interrupted by a bang on the door. Ayesha looked out of her blinds.

"It's yo baby daddy. What? He got someone telling him when you are here?" she questioned.

"That's what it seems like." I said. I opened the door to see what the hell he wanted.

"Yo, how you gon tell me you don't feel good, but yo ass over here?!" He picked up on my vibe and softened his voice.

"Why you been crying Maliah? Where is Aden?" he questioned. I stepped onto the porch and closed the door behind me. I didn't want to bring all of this confusion to Ayesha's doorstep.

"Aden is fine; he is at daycare, and I'm fine. I'm just tired." I said with hopes that he would leave.

"Oh, trouble at home, huh?" he smirked. The last thing I needed was him to be in my business. "I'm fine, Eriq! And don't pull up on me unannounced." I snapped.

"I want to see my baby, and if you over here chillin, it's no reason why I shouldn't be able to see him." he said. "You want to take a ride and clear your mind from whatever the fuck is bothering you?" I knew I should have told him no, but I allowed my vulnerability to lead me to his car. He wasn't driving his G-wagon. We were riding in a clean, old school Cutlass Supreme.

"Don't take me to no local spot." I warned. Even though I was hurt Casey had played me, I didn't want him to see me in public with Eriq without Aden. He didn't respond to my request. Eriq was still handsome as fuck, as I watched him out of the corner of my eye. We drove thirty minutes until we parked in front of an apartment building twenty minutes outside of the city.

"Who lives here?" I asked looking around the area.
"I do, since you won't come home with me, I chill here. I don't like to sit in a big ass empty house alone."

I immediately regretted my decision going anywhere with him after his comment.

"Come on; I'm not going to do anything you don't want to do. We can have a drink and chill until it's time for you to get the kids."

Casey usually picked them up from school during the week, because I would still be at work, but Eriq didn't need to know that. I followed him into the apartment building. It was clean, but nothing special. The inside looked like a typical bachelor pad. I sat on a bar stool while he wasted no time pouring us a drink. He opened the fridge and pulled out a box of pizza.

"Pizza?" He offered holding up the box. I laughed at his gesture.

"No thanks, I'm not hungry." Eriq was always greedy as hell, and it was no telling how long that pizza had been in there.

"Cool, mo for me." He handed me a shot of Hennessy. My mind had been so crowded, and that was just what I needed to take the edge off.

"So what's up? What's bothering you?" he asked, removing the pizza from the microwave.

"I'm cool; I told you I just don't feel well." I said to him pouring me another shot.

"I know you too well. I know when shit ain't right with you. I'm not trying to be in yo business, but if it's something that I can help with, I will."

"It's nothing you can help with. You've done enough, thank you." I sarcastically said. It was because of him my life was in shambles in the first place.

"What the fuck is that supposed to mean?" he asked with his brow raised.

"Just what it sounds like." I sneered.

"If the nigga ain't treating you right, then leave. You ain't waste no time pushin' me to the side when I fucked up."

I didn't know why I allowed myself to be here with him entertaining his petty conversation.

"I don't have time for this shit. Take me to my car." I hopped off the bar stool and was now standing by the door.

"Look, I didn't bring you here for this. I really didn't. I see that you are hurt, and I know I have hurt you, but if I can offer any advice, it would be stop allowing it. You don't deserve to be sad, hurt, none of that shit. You deserve the world for real."

What he was saying was right. I was young and dealing with more shit than a little.

The house Casey bought was beautiful, but I needed my own. I needed to graduate college and find my own way before I poured all of me into a man. This shit had become so draining and had taken over my life.

"I'm good; I don't have trouble in paradise." I joked.

"Yeah, whatever." he laughed.

We drunk a whole pint of Hennessy and talked about crazy shit we did when we were younger. Eriq and I had a lot of history together. He was there when I was dealing with my mama and her addiction. I remembered when I first caught her shooting heroin into her arm, and Eriq had sat on my porch with me that entire night while I cried.

There were nights when we had no food for dinner, and he would bring us sandwiches from his house to eat. I looked back on how far I had come, and despite the bullshit, I was blessed.

He was fucked up laid out on the couch, and we had lost track of time between the shots and the laughter.

"Eriq, get up. I have to go home." I nudged him. It was going on five o'clock pm, and I had to get home to the kids. He reached out for me, pulling me aggressively on top of him. I was drunk my damn self and lost my balance.

"Come on; I have to get going." I repeated.

"You don't want to stay a little longer?" he asked with his eyes closed. I didn't move from off top of him.

My head was spinning, and I just needed to lay there. I felt him rubbing my ass, and his dick was hard underneath me. I didn't attempt to stop him; I continued to lay there.

"If you tell me to stop, I'll stop Maliah." his words were slow.

I looked up at his face, and he looked back at me and smiled. He pulled my face up to kiss me. I know I should have stopped him, just like I know I shouldn't have left with him and came there to begin with, but I kissed him back. We were both consumed with alcohol and untamed emotions, and he wasted no time stripping us both.

I felt a rush of air as he picked me up and pinned me to the wall. I wrapped my legs around him as he entered me. I closed my eyes as I rode him standing up. My ass was cupped in the palm of his hands as he pulled me into his thrusts.

The feeling felt so familiar, before all of the confusion began in my life. Although it felt familiar, it also felt wrong. I was in love with another man.

"I'm sorry." he whispered. Tears fell down my face, because I knew I had just made life worse for myself. I closed my eyes and came all over Eriq before everything went black.

I opened my eyes, and my head was spinning, so I squinted my eyes to help get my vision focused. I checked my surroundings, and I was in Ayesha's living room.

"No, no, no." I panicked to myself. I had awaken to my worse nightmare.

Casey was standing in the doorway, and Ayesha was standing next to him with a smirk on her face. I tried to process my thoughts.

The last thing I remembered was laying on top of Eriq. *God no.* I thought.

Casey's face was tight, and the vein in his neck was protruding.

"What is going on?" I asked confused. I looked down at my chest, and I had bite marks and hickeys all over my cleavage.

"She ain't nothing but a hoe." Ayesha spat.

"Hoe?" I stood up and charged at her. "You bitch!!" I yelled. It didn't take long for me to put the situation together. She had called Casey here, just like she told him about all the other shit he mysteriously knew about.

"Casey, I don't know what she told you, but you need to hear me out." I pleaded as he stood between the both of us.

"Were you with him?" he asked.

"With who?" I knew who he was referring to but I didn't want to answer him.

It was crazy how this all flipped on me when I had seen him with my eyes ignore my call when he was with his baby mama.

"Yes, Casey, but I don't know what happened. I was drinking and-.""

"GET IN THE FUCKIN CAR!!" he roared. I wanted to punch Ayesha in her shit.

I didn't know what her motive was. I had never done shit to her for her to turn on me and not have my back, but I scurried to his car, looking around for mine.

Where the fuck is my car? How did I get back to Ayesha's? I thought.

The car ride home was gruesome. He didn't say one word to me, but the tension was intense. The house was empty when we got there, and it was two o'clock in the morning on a weekday.

"Did you fuck him!?" he yelled in my face.

"No… I don't know, Casey." I cried sliding to the floor.

"You don't know?!" he began breaking shit all through the house.

He walked up to me and squeezed my face so hard with his hand I felt the lining of my jaw cut on my teeth, so I kicked him in the leg, so he could let me go.

"Get the fuck off of me! Don't touch me; blame yourself! You were too busy laid up with your bitch to worry about me! I saw you, Casey. I saw you leave her house and ignore my phone call! I was there." I cried in his face. "The question is did you fuck her!?" I wasn't allowing him to assassinate my character without him owning up to his own shit.

Two wrongs didn't make a right, but both parties needed to be addressed here.

He stood there and said nothing.

"Did you fuck her?! I asked again. "Better yet, are you fucking her?" I rephrased the question. I had been having the feeling that he was cheating on me for a while now.

"Yeah, I'm fuckin her." he responded.

"Well, I guess that means we both ain't shit then Casey." I said to him walking to the bedroom.

I packed as many clothes as I could and I left. It fucked me up that Ayesha set me up like this, and I made a mental note to beat her ass when I caught up with her.

I was tired and suffering from a hangover, so I checked into a hotel nearby to catch up on some sleep and figure things out. I soaked in the hotel's bathtub and replayed my visit with Eriq.

When did I get home? I had so many unanswered questions.

I called Eriq with hopes of finding out what exactly happened. It was now five in the morning.

"Hello" he answered the phone half asleep.

"Eriq, it's me. Did you drive me back to Ayesha's house?" I asked him.

"Nah, she came and got you. I was too fucked up drive." he said.

I was even more amped to beat her ass. She could have helped cover for me, but she called Casey. I replayed times in my head when she was always on she jealous shit since I moved out the hood.

Hating ass bitches. I thought.

"You cool?" he asked more alert than when he answered the phone.

"Yeah, I'm cool. Thanks." I said hanging up.

Over the course of the week, I was busy with moving my things from Casey's condo. He was still never there, but I was over it. It just kept him out of my way while I handled my business.

I found a three-bedroom ranch for us to live in until I found something better. The kids were not happy that we were breaking up, but I explained to them that they would still see Casey. For the past year, he was the closest thing they had ever had to an extended family, and I wasn't going to take that from them.

My mama was still going strong in rehab, and I couldn't have been happier for her. The visitations with Eriq were awkward now for me. We never talked about what happened that night, but we both were aware of what went down. Marquita was lucky to have been away; she wasn't in the mist of all the bullshit.

Aden's 1st birthday party was finally this weekend, and I hadn't talked to Casey to see if he was coming. I sat on my kitchen counter sipping wine and unpacking my kitchenware. The few days I had been in my new house, I had to admit it felt better than when I was living at the condo. It was a fresh start, and I felt accomplished that I had did it on my own.

Eriq had offered me six thousand dollars, but I declined. Although three thousand of it was mine, I just didn't feel comfortable taking anything from him, and I simply didn't need it. Sam Smith sung his heart out through my Bluetooth speakers as I cleaned the house.

"Maliah." Kayla called out to me, breaking my groove. I looked at her giving her my full attention.

"I miss Casey." she whined. This was her every day struggle since we moved.

She hadn't seen him in three days, and it was killing her. I knew that our break-up was going to be hard on them, because although he would still be in their lives, it wouldn't be as much as it was before. I missed him, too, but clearly, he didn't want me anymore. He was with Bridgette.

I wasn't going to beg him to stay or cry over him leaving. I was going to focus on getting my shit together. Feeling sorry for my little sister, I texted him.

Me: Hey, Kayla misses you.

When he didn't respond to my text, I instantly regretted sending it. He clearly wasn't missing us as much as we were missing his black ass. I did something that had become my new profound hobby, and that was logging into Facebook to check Bridgette's page.

I needed to see if she had any recent posts about Casey since he had become so distant with me. I hated the fact that I cared so much. I had a daily prayer that I would find closure in leaving his ass in the past, but I was coming up short with that request. I typed her name in the search field, and immediately, I noticed that she had updated her profile picture. I tapped on the picture to get an up close view and it was a picture of her hand with a fat ass rock sitting on her ring finger. I scrolled through the comments, and everyone was telling her congratulations, including Mrs. Rice.

My hands began to shake, as I continued to look at pics of her and Casey hugging after what appeared to be a proposal. I had experienced my fair share of pain in the past, but this topped it all.

"That bitch ass nigga." I said to myself. I couldn't believe he had played me like that. I was starting to think that these niggas took me as some sort of joke.

He was just in my ear about moving together in a house to raise our family, but he was about to make this bitch his wife in sure a short period of time after our break up. I couldn't deal. He was more uncertain about his feelings than a female.

I wanted nothing more than the both of them dead. I was tired of being made a fool out of. It was true enough that I cheated on him with Eriq, but prior to that incident happening, he was already creeping with her behind my back. As I contemplated thoughts of them being wiped off the earth, my phone alerted me that a text came through.

Casey: I miss them, too. Tell her I will pick her up from school tomorrow.

I relayed the message to her, and she was dancing all over the house. It bothered me that he didn't have too much to say to me, and I wanted to ask him about this engagement, but I decided to grow up. If he wanted that ugly ass female as his wife, then so be it. I pushed all of the ill feelings to the side.

It was time for Maliah to live for Maliah.

Chapter 18: Maliah

"Happy Birthday to youuuu! Happy Birthday to youuu! Happy Birthday dear Aden, Happy Birthday to youuuu!"

Everyone sang in unison. He was being a brat today. He didn't want anyone holding him, nor did he want to play any of the arcade games. My mama, Marquita, Shawnie, and a few other ladies I went to school with and their kids were there. Jaylen and Kayla ran around having fun, and I hadn't talked to Casey. From the looks of it, he wasn't coming.

If I had known that he was not coming, I would have invited Eriq rather than let him have a separate gathering for my baby, but I just wanted to keep the peace. As I mingled with everyone while they ate cake and ice cream, Casey and Mrs. Rice walked through the door. Mrs. Rice was holding Baby Cailey in her arms, and Casey was bearing gifts. Aden damn near hit the floor trying to get out of my arms to get to him.

"Dada." he yelled. He was never that excited to see me.

"Happy Birthday, A!" Casey picked Aden up after setting the gifts on the gift table.

"Hi, Maliah." Mrs. Rice spoke.

"Hi, how are you?" I asked.

"I'm good, couldn't be better." she said taking a seat. She was very nice to me since Casey and I weren't together.

"Hello everyone." Casey spoke out to all of the guests. Everyone waved and nodded to him, then he walked over closer to me.

"Hey, what's good?" he asked me. My eyes were roaming all over him. I don't think he ever had bad days. No matter what, he was always best dressed and fine as fuck. I shrugged my shoulders at his question.

"You look nice" he said smiling. I tried to refrain from smiling at his compliment, but I couldn't resist.

"We just sang Happy Birthday. I was going to open gifts with him, but he's tired." I said.

"Come here; I want you to see the baby. After keeping her from me for six months, I didn't think I would ever see her besides on pictures. He swapped Aden for Cailey with Mrs. Rice. She was sleeping, but even in her sleep, she was beautiful with her soft, curly hair, and glowing mocha skin. I was still upset about him asking Bridgette to marry him, but I had to keep my composure at my son's birthday party.

"She's beautiful, Casey." I told him getting emotional. I could never be bitter towards a child, especially his child. The way he loved my son and my siblings was a true blessing. He cared for each of them as if they were his own.

"Thank you. Sorry it took so long for you to see her." he apologized.

"It's cool; I'm sure you had your reasons." I was almost certain Bridgette was in his ear telling him not to bring her around me.

The remaining time spent at the party was a great time. Everyone was getting along and I could not have asked for a better turn-out for him. When the party was over, Casey told Mrs. Rice that he was riding back to my house with me to help unload Aden's gifts. He didn't ask me first before making these arrangements, but I had missed his company, so I didn't argue it. Mrs. Rice was going to take Cailey back to Bridgette's house.

The kids were excited that he was coming home with us, but I didn't like that idea of him coming around them and then leaving again for weeks. They had accepted the fact that they would see him mostly during the week when he was picking them up from school.

"So what have you been into?" he asked breaking the silence as I drove.

"School and work, the usual." I said dry as possible. I was bitter that he went back to Bridgette. I stayed stalking her Facebook page to see posts about Casey.

"What have you been into?" I wanted to know why he was in the car with me and what was he expecting to come from this.

"I've been straight; just workin... hustling," he said looking out the window.

I wanted to ask him why did he leave me to go back to her, but I did not want to have that conversation with him in front of the kids, so I would save that for another time.

When we got to the house, all of the kids were sleeping and worn out from the birthday party, so we carried them into the house, along with all of the leftover party supplies without saying two words to each other.

"Why are you here Casey? I'm appreciative of you coming to Aden's party."

He sat on the couch holding Aden while he slept in his arms. "I came over to talk to you, and to see what's going on with you moving into the house." I couldn't believe that he was still talking about a damn house.

He had a whole bitch at home, but he was still trying to get me under his roof.

"I'm not moving in that house, Casey. I am working on getting things together for myself without your help. Like, you for real have your nerve to ask me to live in a house that you bought, and you have a fiancé!! You think that you are about to bounce back and forth from me to her, you are crazy as hell. And you really crazy if you think that I'm about to play a side bitch to her." I said, throwing my hands up in the air out of frustration.

I got even more annoyed with him sitting there with a dumbass smirk on his face.

"Are you done? I'm not trying to bounce back and forth between shit. I haven't been messing with that girl like that. I did propose to her, but a nigga came to his senses quick. I was trying cope with my pain in ways I would regret forever."

A part of me felt like he was full of shit, but another part felt relieved to hear him say he wasn't involved with her on that level.

"So you are sitting here telling me that you don't live with her? That you're not in a relationship with her? That y'all aren't getting married?" I was not about to allow him to play me like a fool.

"No to all of those questions, man. I'm here asking you can I have my family all under one roof. I mean, I'm being one hunnit with you. She's been down for a nigga for a long time, and we got Cailey together, but I don't love her like that." he sighed.

I was not about to run back to him just because his shit didn't work out as planned. Bridgette could have his ass for all I cared.

"No, I'm good, Casey. I don't want to live with you. I just want to get me right.

"I'm telling you part of getting you together is bringing us back together. I am not fuckin with her no more. I allowed that shit with you and that nigga to cloud my judgment. I know that you don't believe shit I'm saying, but I stopped fuckin with the bitch cuz she has control issues, and I'm in love with you. I'on want these silly broads out here." I was hearing him, but I had been hurt too many times to be putting myself right back in a vulnerable position.

"I'm tired, and I really don't want to hear what it is that you have to say." I had made up my mind, and I was not getting sucked in by his fine ass sitting on my couch pouring out his heart.

"Yeah okay; as long as you hear me is what matters." he said walking over to the kitchen counter to cut him a piece of birthday cake.

I sat on the couch, and on the table was his phone vibrating off the hook. I picked it up thinking that he would be on my head for touching it, but to my surprise, he didn't say anything at all. When I saw that it was Bridgette, I debated on being petty or putting the phone back down, but I couldn't resist being petty, so I answered it.

"Hello," I answered. She was silent for a good minute before she responded.

"Why the fuck are you answering Case's phone?" she asked, with a nasty tone.

"The question here is why are you blowing his phone up? He is spending time with his son." I said as calm as possible.

"Bitch, that's not even his son. Can you put Case on the phone? I need to talk to him about his daughter!" she yelled into the phone.

"I just told yo ass that he busy, now unless it's life or death, he will call you later." I hung up in her face.

She needed to know that she did not run shit. It was true enough that she was the mother of his biological child, but my son was just as well his as Cailey was in his eyes, and if she had a problem with it, then she needed to talk to Casey about it.

"Now was that necessary? Did it make you feel better?" he asked, while stuffing his mouth with cake.

"Actually, it did. I'm sick of her ass." I said, walking to my bedroom. Shit, I was tired of his ass, too. I showered and got under my sheets. Dealing with all of those kids at the party had me worn out. I was over all of these muthafuckas. It didn't take long after I was in bed for Casey to come in to join me. Although he was the reason that I was stressed out, I still wanted him to relieve my stress. I did not deny him when he got into the bed and had no clothes on. My body had been missing the shit out of him, and I was ready.

I felt his masculine hands rub up and down the small of the back, and my body locked up from his touch. He then used both of his hands to massage my shoulders.

"Mmmm, that feels good," I moaned into the pillow. He laid his body over top of mine and used fingers to massage my clit while tracing my neckline with his tongue. I felt my climax build up with every flick of his finger.

Before my body reached its peak, he was entering me from the back. Upon entering, he used his free hand to push my head into the pillow to muffle my cries.

I felt every inch of him, as he used his weight to dig deep into me. There was no way I would ever be able to get over this feeling that he was giving me.

"I missed you," he breathed into my ear. I didn't want to open my mouth to respond. I was already struggling to keep quiet and not wake the kids.

He continued to thrust his body into mine, until I felt the beads of sweat drip onto the back of my neck. He abruptly stopped to flip me over aggressively and guided me on top of him, then I straddled him and adjusted my position to ride.

Our fingers locked as I closed my eyes and enjoyed every bit of the ecstasy that I was feeling. He unlocked his hands with me to hold me by the waist and forcefully meet my body with hard powerful stokes. My words were backed up in my throat, and my body went completely numb as the temperature in the room went up.

"I'm cumming, Baby." Just as the words escaped my mouth, I came all over him. He increased his speed, and it was not long before he joined me in pleasure.

I knew in my heart that I did not want to let him go, but I also didn't understand where I fit at in his life.

Chapter 19: Case

Spending time with Maliah and the kids had me realizing how much I had missed them. I was doing so much to keep busy and keep my mind off of the pain that I had felt from us breaking up.

I learned real quickly that there was no walking out of love, and the best thing to do was to embrace it. What I battled with the most was that it was hard for me to talk to her about how happy she was that Rosie was trying to get clean.

Of course, I couldn't tell her that her mama was a dead woman walking. I wouldn't expect her to understand the street code when it came to her mama. But I was getting harassed by cops left and right because of her ass.

Yesterday, I had a police car staked outside of my barbershop all day. I knew it was only a matter of time before they knew that I wasn't the one that would lead them to shit and start to fuck with my moms, dad, and brothers. It was hard to get a hold of Rosie with her being in that rehabilitation center, but I knew that it was only a matter of time before she was back on the streets.

I had a meeting today on the eastside of Detroit to buy up a few properties that in the neighborhood, and afterwards, I was going to take Maliah somewhere and romance her. That was something that I had been wanting to do, but my pride wasn't set up like that. All I could think about was that nigga being with her after I had made her mine.

I still had him on my hit list. The nigga was always out of dodge, but if he knew what was best for him, that's how he should keep it.

Driving down 75 South toward Detroit brought back memories that I had as kid taking this trip every weekend. My pops was from Flint, so when him and my mama first got together, we would all link up every weekend there. That lasted for years until they got married, and we eventually moved to Flint. My heart will forever be with my city. The eastside was where I got the most hoes, built the best friendships, and made the most money.

Later on that evening, when I was done cutting checks throughout the city, I made my way to my old hood to see my homie Tray. The hood looked nothing like it did when I lived there. It now looked like the slums, and if you weren't from there, you damn sure couldn't see no beauty within the abandoned houses, which once housed my friends, or the trashed streets that I used to ride my bike and play basketball in.

As I was pulling up on Tray, my phone vibrated. I looked at my screen, and it was Shawnie. She never called me; I believe that was for real the first time.

"Fuck she won't," I said to myself. "Hello?"

"Case, where are you? You need to get here quick!! Maliah was in a fight!" she screamed into my ear.

I drove passed Tray's house with my foot heavy on the gas. This shit would happen when I was far from home.

"A fight with who?!" I tried to remain calm as possible.

"I don't know; I was on my way to the store when my sister called and told me that she seen a bunch of cop cars and ambulances at the attorney's office where Maliah works. I drove by and saw them put her in the back of the ambulance. Bystanders told me that she was in a fight with two girls and a man came and broke it up. She's at McLaren."

I hung up on her. I didn't want to hear any more details about the shit. I needed to be there. I was enraged, but I knew that I had a long drive to Flint, and I had to make it in one piece and not get into a car accident. *Who in the fuck would go to her job and go after her?* I thought.

My mind went to Bridgette. She wasn't dumb enough to pull a stunt like this, but you couldn't put shit past anyone these days. I called her just to see if I could rule her out.

"Hey Case," she answered on the first ring.

"Where you at?!" I snapped at her out of anger.

"I'm at home with my daughter where I should be. Case. I ain't talked to you all day, and you call me with an attitude. I'm taking Cailey tonight, and we are going to move with my mama in Illinois. I can't continue to stay here and go through this stress."

"You got me fucked up! My daughter better be there when I get there!" She was still in her feelings about me letting Maliah meet Cailey. I didn't care about her feelings, but she was going to feel it if she thought leaving town with my baby was going to happen.

"Case, I'm leaving tonight."

I hung up on here ass, too. I couldn't get to Flint fast enough.

Chapter 20: Maliah

The following weeks were hard for me to get into a routine. I had to commend single mothers because juggling three kids while trying to work and go to school was hard. I couldn't depend much on Eriq to help with Aden because he too busy in the streets. Anything I needed from him financially, he was there, but every time I looked up, he was leaving out of state or MIA for a week. He grew up piss poor, so now that he was making fast money, he had become addicted and was definitely on a path of self-destruction.

We argued constantly about Casey spending time with Aden. They had been in several confrontations since the club incident, and I wished that they both realized Aden was all that mattered at this point before they killed one another.

I sat at my office desk filtering through Cases and came across a file that had the name Gino Rice across the front of it. When I saw the name Gino, a chill ran down my back. The only thing I could envision was that monster swinging my mama around the house like she was a rag doll. I opened the manila folder and the case formed against him was for identity theft. After reading the notes more in detail, the attorney that I worked for was trying to get him off charges for identity theft and real estate fraud.

I was hoping that I could find a picture to see if this was the same person that attacked us, but I didn't find a picture. I did find a schedule that notified me that a meeting was scheduled here at the office with him next Tuesday. I stored the appointment in my phone. If this was the same person, and we were fighting his case at my job, then I was making it my business for his ass to be locked up and put away for good.

I took my blazer off of the back of my office chair and was ready to call it a night. I had put in enough time in the office, and I was ready to get home and kick back.

My boss hated for me to leave the office late at night by myself, but I was determined to finish all of my work. That way, I could have my weekend to do what I wanted. I armed the security code to the building and walked out to my car. As soon as I walked out, I had this eerie feeling that something was not right. I began to speed up my pace, because my car was not parked that far from the door.

When I finally made it to my car, I regretted my decision on staying late. There was a brick through the windshield of my car, and someone had went to work on my car with a bat. My mind immediately drifted to Bridgette. I pulled out my cell phone to call Casey when I was hit over the head with an object. I held out my hands in from in front of me to break my fall. Blood began to run down my face, and my head was spinning. I looked up, and with blurred vision, I saw Ayesha and April.

Apparently, it took both of these hating bitches to come for me. The sad part about it was I never did a thing to either of these hoes. I kicked Ayesha as hard as I could in her shin with my six-inch heels, and her fat ass came down to her knees off that one. I was not moving as fast as I would have liked to, but it was fast enough to get back on my feet and punch April in her face.

I continued to deliver blows to her face while Ayesha was still down. April was no match for me, even with my vision impaired from the blood pouring from my head. I was so busy beating the shit out of April, I didn't notice Ayesha sneak up alongside of me and hit me in my rib cage with a bat. I had a death grip on April's hair, but I immediately released it when the bat hit my side. I knew that I was losing a lot of blood, because I was starting to slip in and out of consciousness. My eyelids began to feel heavy before they completely closed, then I saw a dark, tall shadow standing over me, and the kicks I was feeling stopped.

Everything went pitch black against my will.

Chapter 21: Maliah

I woke up to a bandage over my head and a headache that hurt so bad it made me wish I didn't wake up. *What the fuck happened to me?* I thought.

Just as I tried to get out of the hospital bed, a nurse came into the room to stop me.

"No, sweetie, you have to relax. What do you need? I will get it." she asked politely.

"How did I get here?" I asked, closing my eyes, because the bright light was causing my head to pound harder.

"You were physically assaulted in a parking lot on Tuesday night." she informed me.

"Physically assaulted? On Tuesday?" I asked her for confirmation.

"Yes, sweetheart."

"What day is it?" I was confused, and I didn't like the way that it felt.

"It's Thursday."

"I'm going to go get the doctor and let him know that you are awake. I will also get you something for pain to help you relax."

My entire body was pained, and I couldn't move anything without hurting. As she went to get the doctor, I laid there trying to figure out who attacked me. My last memory was being at work. I continued to wrack my brain until it hit me. I laid there and relived the entire fight.

"It was Ayesha and April who did this me" I whispered to myself.

I was in the hospital away from kids that had no one but me because of two jealous bitches that I hadn't done a thing to. I wanted to snatch the IV out of my arm and go hunt them down.

Casey walked into the room interrupting my vicious thoughts. He was holding a bouquet of Roses and a card. He looked stressed out. His clothes were wrinkled, and his eyes were red. He looked like he had been awake for two days straight. He sat the flowers on the stand next to me and kissed my bandaged forehead.

"I'm so thankful that you are okay." he said sitting next to me.

"I know who did this Case." I whispered to him.

I didn't want anyone to hear me. I wanted to take care of these bitches personally.

"I know, too. You need to get some rest. I got this covered."

I believed him. Casey was a protector, and he hated for his family or niggas to be fucked with. Everyone around him would be good if he could help it.

I had to spend the next two days in the hospital until I was discharged to go home. Casey tried to convince me to go home with him, but I refused. The more I thought about them jumping me, the angrier I also became with him. I kept having flashbacks of them standing side by side when I got busted at her house after sleeping with Eriq. I wanted to put a hit out on all of these muthafuckas.

~~~~~~~~~~~~

Three weeks went by since the fight happened, and I had not been out to see anyone. Bridgette had dipped off without a trace, and it had Casey losing his mind. She told him that she was going to stay with her mama, but he flew out to Illinois, and there wasn't a sign that she had been there. Her mama told him that she hadn't talked to Bridgette in months. I was kind of relieved that he didn't find her, because he was so angry and hurt that I couldn't say that he wouldn't have hurt her. All of her social media accounts she had had been deactivated, and she had a new number.

Shawnie had stopped by to visit me earlier and told me how the police had been going to Mrs. Rice's house frequently, and she left her house and went into hiding, with hopes that they would lay off of the investigation. Casey hadn't mentioned his mama moving to me, but I had noticed how his whole demeanor had changed. He seemed to always be on high alert and paranoid.

It was late, and I finally had some alone time to myself with everyone sleep. Marquita had come home to help me out since I suffered a fractured rib cage and had staples in my head. I sat in my bed watching Menace to Society on HBO. No Matter how much I was telling myself that I was preparing to leave Casey in my past, my mind kept wondering to thoughts of him. I badly missed the way we were when we first started out. I was determined to keep us at a distance and the only common ground between us would be the kids. I was too damaged from the stories that I had heard about him and Bridgette parading around the city together. Apparently, life with her was far less complicated than it was with me since he kept going back.

My thoughts were interrupted by a knock on my door. It was late, and I was not expecting company. That was one of the downsides to living alone. I was always nervous that someone would try to break in. I didn't want Marquita going to the door alone, so I made her help me out of bed to answer it. I looked through my peephole and saw a police officer at my door.

"How can I help you?!" I yelled through the door. I didn't trust people, and the police was definitely not an exception.

"I'm looking for Maliah Andrews." He said.

"How can I help you?" I repeated.

"It's in regards to Rosemary Andrews, ma'am"." Hearing my mom's name made me instantly drop my guards. I opened the door and was face to face with a white policeman.

"I'm Maliah. What about Rosemary?" I asked feeling myself becoming frantic. The officer removed his hat. "No." I mumble shaking my head.

My biggest fear was becoming reality.

"I'm sorry, Maliah. Your mother discharged herself from rehabilitation two days ago, and we found her body today in a nearby alley. The cause of death is unknown, but it is believed to be from a drug overdose." His words were becoming distant.

I could no longer hear anything that he was saying. This could not be happening. I had just seen my mom last week, and she was clean and healthy.

Why would she give in and allow herself to be defeated? I thought. I cried as the officer left my door step.

"Oh God, why?" I cried. I must have been loud, because Jaylen came running into the kitchen where I was sitting on the floor with Marquita. I didn't care about how much pain that I was in physically. My mother was gone, and she was never coming back.

"What's wrong sis?" he asked concern. I didn't know how I was going to tell them that our mother was dead.

We all had hopes that she was on her way to becoming the mother that we always needed her to be, and then this tragedy happened. I explained to Jaylen the news that the police officer had shared with me, and there was no calming him down. He cried hysterically. So many thoughts raced through my mind. What didn't set well with me was the fact my mom had been making so much progress. It was devastating to know that she relapsed. I called the first person that came to mind, Casey. I knew that I could depend on him to help me console the kids and get this all figured out.

He answered after the first couple of rings. "Yo, what's up?" he asked into the phone. I could not stop the tears from falling from my eyes.

"Casey, my mom is dead." I whimpered to him.

"Dead? Aw shit, I'm sorry to hear that."

"Where are you?" I asked. I knew that he would be at my house before I could even hang up from him good.

"I just left the airport; I'll be heading your way."

Casey got to my house within two hours. He came in the door asking me question after question, mostly ones I did not have the answer to. We eased Jaylen's mind the best we could, because he needed to get some sleep, and I needed to do the same. I knew I had my day cut out beginning first thing in the morning with identifying my mama's body.

I fell asleep that night crying in Casey's arms. It felt reassuring that I had him in my corner, even throughout our own personal issues. This was the hardest time I had to face in my life.

Over the next couple of days, I had many things to figure out. My mother didn't have life insurance, so I had to cover all of her funeral arrangements and expenses.

Jaylen, Kayla, and Aden had been staying with Mrs. Rice, while I managed to handle everything. I stopped by the rehabilitation center where she was before the incident to get all of her belongings.

"Hi Maliah, I'm so sorry for your lost." one of the nurses on staff said to me.

"Thank you; I appreciate your condolences." I said to her as I was going through my mom's dresser drawers.

The nurse stepped back into the room. "You know, I really didn't trust that young kid that came up here. He didn't seem to have your mom's best interest at heart, but I understood that family is family." she said.

I had no idea who she was referencing, because we didn't have no damn family.

"What kid, Ms. Patty?" I questioned.

"Chile I'm not good with names." she said shaking her head.

"May I see all of my mom's visitation sign-ins since she's been here please?

"Sure, you have all access since you was her caretaker. I'll go gather them." I continued going through her things.

I came across pictures of us all growing up throughout the years. The pictures brought tears to my eyes. When my mother wasn't high, she was such a beautiful person with a huge giving heart.

"Here you are, baby." Ms. Patty said upon entering the room.

I retrieved the sign-in forms from her hand, and she left the room. I sat in a nearby chair and began thumbing through the forms. The first few pages only had signatures from Marquita and me. I reached the third page and a lump formed in my throat. Eriq's signature was throughout the remaining pages. I reached the last visitation log and saw that he was the last visitor before her death.

Why has he been visiting my mama? I thought. I immediately ransacked my purse looking for my phone to call him, but his phone went straight to voicemail.

I tried to come up with a reason as to why would Eriq would be visiting my mama, and I came up short. The nurses told me that his visits were always short, and my mom had confrontations with him before in the past where he was escorted out of the facility.

I talked to him frequently, and he had never mentioned anything to me about visiting her. I called Marquita to enlighten her on my discovery.

"Hello." she answered.

"I was just getting mama's things from the rehab, and on the visitation log was Eriq's name." My hands were shaking as I talked to her.

If Eriq had anything to do with my mama dying, he was a dead man.

"What? Why would he be visiting her?" she questioned.

"My point exactly. I have been trying to reach him but I can't get ahold of him."

"That's not adding up. Do you think he had something to do with all of this?" she asked.

"I don't know, Quita, but I sure as hell will find out. I will keep you posted when I hear something."

I debated with myself if I was going to tell Casey. I didn't want to burden him with my problems and business, and he wasn't even my man. His family was helping me enough with the kids.

I tried to call Eriq again, and this time, he answered.

"Yo, what's going on?" he answered coolly.

"Eriq, why in the fuck were you visiting my mama at rehab?" I wasted no time asking his ass.

I had a headache trying to make sense of the situation. There was a moment of silence before he responded.

"Meet me on Fenton; I can explain the shit." he said nonchalantly.

"I'm not meeting you no damn where. You're going to explain now. I was not traveling across the city for him to tell me something he could say over the phone.

"If yo ass want to know, you will meet me there. Otherwise, I'm not talking to you about shit over the phone." And with that he hung up.

"Muthafucka." I mumbled looking at my phone. I was frustrated the entire drive to Fenton. He often hung out in that area for whatever reason.

I was starting to despise Eriq. He was becoming sketchier as time went on, and I was starting to second guess his motives since the day I met him. I drove down Fenton street until I saw him standing on the corner with a group of niggas shooting dice.

Once he saw me pull up, he dismissed himself from the game. The sun had went down, and the street was dark.

"Come holla at me." he said opening my car door.

"Eriq, I don't need to be doing all of that. I just want to know what the fuck is going on!" I had lost all patience with him.

"Would you come on and chill in the car and talk to me?"

"You can sit in my car." I snapped.

"I'm not sitting in a car that nigga bought you." he said with his face twisted.

Annoyed with him, I got out of my car and walked across the street to his truck.

Once we were in, he looked at me and said, "Your mama was in some real shit. She stole some drugs from the wrong person. I was trying to help her and pay off the niggas she stole from, but she insisted on not being serious about it. I guess she thought by going to rehab it would wash away the mistake she made." He sparked a blunt and took a hit.

"What? Who did she steal from?" I asked trying to make sense of his story.

"Gino." he said taking another hit.

Gino. I thought. I was tired of hearing this nigga's name. He had caused more problems in my life than a little.

"Why didn't you tell me Eriq? I could have helped her." I cried.

"Trust me, you helped her more than you know." he mumbled.

"Where is the nigga, Gino? How did he kill her?" I needed to know more.

"I don't know, Maliah. She wanted me to stay away and act like the shit would go away after I tried to help her." he hung his head down.

"I don't fuckin believe you!!" I screamed punching him in his arm. He grabbed my hands to stop the blows from coming at him.

"I would never hurt you purposely or kill your fuckin mama!" he shouted. "Mrs. Rice's husband is Gino." he said.

"Mrs. Rice?" I asked, looking at him with bewilderment.

"Yea, you heard me." he said, as I processed what he had just told me.

"He killed my mama?" I mumbled.

"My kids were at his house, while I was planning my mama's funeral." I was getting sick to my stomach.

"Did Casey know this shit?" I didn't know if I could believe anything Eriq was telling me, but my gut instinct told me that he was telling the truth.

"He don't have much to do with this drug game. As much as I don't like the nigga, I gotta be real and say he always tried to look out for your moms, so I don't think he had shit do with it." Eriq said shaking his head.

Mrs. Rice had to have known. I thought. I only saw Mr. Rice on a few occasions. He was always out of town on business, and that definitely was not the same man that attacked my mama at our house. He sent others to do his dirty work.

"I have to go Eriq." I said opening his passenger door.

"Maliah, I want you to keep Aden away from all those mutherfuckas. I want him out of dodge." Eriq warned.

As I was getting ready to get out of the car, when another car was slowly approaching us head on with no headlights on. Everything about the car looked suspicious. My car was parked a few houses down, and I didn't feel comfortable walking to it.

"Get back in the car!" Eriq yelled.

As soon as I did, bullets started pinging at Eriq's truck. It all was happening so fast that I thought I was going to die because of how fast my heart was racing. Eriq was ducking low with me and shooting back. The bullets got in close range, so I peeked up and a masked gun man was standing on the driver's side of the car with a gun aimed at Eriq. My entire life flashed before my eyes. Images of Aden, Kayla, Marquita, and Jaylen's face appeared.

I began to pray that they would be looked after without me, because I knew that my life would not be spared tonight. My hands trembled on my lap, and I realized they were covered in blood. The gunman let off several rounds in Eriq's body before I fainted.

"Hey, Mama." I said to mother.

Her skin glowed under the sunlight, and she was so vibrant and healthy.

"Hi, my beautiful Maliah." she chimed.

"I'm so sorry, Mama. I had no idea they were trying to hurt you." I cried embracing her.

"It's okay; it was my wrongs that I couldn't undo I don't want you to dwell on me. You have made me the proudest mother, and I know that I failed you, your sisters and brother, but you still loved me and never gave up on me.

Thank you, Maliah. Live your life and be the absolute best in all you do." she said hugging me. Her body was ice cold, and although I had heard every word that she was telling me, I knew that it was too late. My fate was already determined, and all I could do was have faith that the kids would be okay and would always remember everything that I had taught them.

"It's not your time, Baby Girl, but when it is, I will be right here waiting for you. I love you." Her body broke into tiny pieces, and the sunlight went away leaving me alone. Life had been hard on me, but I had to continue to fight. I still had a long journey to go.

Chapter 22: Maliah

I sat on a hospital bed for the second time in less than a month. Only this time, I was numb. I didn't feel an ounce of pain. All that I could envision was me frantically shaking Eriq's lifeless body to wake up, but he never did. I had lost my mama and my child's father. The doctor held a light up to my eye causing me to remember to blink.

Policemen filled the halls of the hospital waiting to question me on what I had witnessed. While all I wanted was to wake up from this nightmare, I couldn't help but to feel like I was still being punished for something cruel that I had done.

I replayed Eriq's conversation with me over and over again in my mind. *Gino, was behind hurting and killing my mama.* I thought.

"I have to go get my kids!" I snapped out of the depression I was drowning in.

"They are in the waiting area, Maliah." the doctor said to me.

"I need to see them; I need to hug them." I hopped off of the bed and walked toward the door.

The doctor nodded to the nurse that it was okay to let me go. The guard escorted me to the area they were in. One of the police officers asked me if I was okay to give a statement, and I told him no. I didn't know anything besides Eriq was dead, and I'm sure they had that part figured out by now. I also knew that the hitter knew not to kill me. It didn't make sense.

It was dark outside, but I saw them pause with hesitation and then they killed Eriq.

Eriq's story had some truth to it, and that was exactly why he had to die. He knew too much, and with my mama dead, they couldn't risk keeping him alive. I needed to talk to Case. He was the only person that could help me put this all together or even make me feel a little better other than the kids.

When I got to the waiting area, I was greeted by their tired, smiling faces. Marquita was sleeping in a chair, and Shawnie walked up to hug me.

"I had to go and get the kids. Mrs. Rice went down to the police station. Case was taken into custody for Eriq's murder." she whispered so the kids couldn't hear her.

I stared in her eyes with tears welled up, and she nodded her head yes to give me confirmation of her words.

Was this the ultimate price I had to pay for loving a hustla?
TO BE CONTINUED...........

For more information on how to help with the city of Flint's water crisis please visit

www.helpforflint.com

SUBMISSION GUIDELINES

Silver Dynasty Publications is currently accepting submissions. Send the first 3 chapters of your manuscript in a word document, a synopsis, and contact information to silverdynastypublications@yahoo.com for consideration.

CPSIA information can be obtained
at www.ICGtesting.com
Printed in the USA
LVHW051658011020
667693LV00010B/965